STREETCAR MAN

This life-size bronze statue of Thomas Lowry, situated at Hennepin Avenue and Twenty-Fourth Street in Minneapolis, bears a remarkable resemblance to its subject. Its creator, the distinguished Austrian sculptor Karl Bitter, found a man with a build like Lowry's and had him pose in Lowry's clothing. In the eyes of Lowry's friends, the result came close to reincarnation.

STREETCAR MAN

Tom Lowry and the
Twin City Rapid Transit Company

Goodrich Lowry

Lerner Publications Company
Minneapolis

PHOTO ACKNOWLEDGMENTS: The photographs have been reproduced through the courtesy of : p. ii, Duane Braley; pp. 5, 15 (bottom), 18, 49, 61, 111 (*Harper's Weekly*), 132, 140, 151, 152, Goodrich Lowry; pp. 10, 11, 15 (top), 64, 141, 143, Minneapolis Public Library and Information Center; pp. 22 (Jacoby photo), 32 (Sweet photo), 41, 44 (Minneapolis Public Library and Information Center), 68, 73 (Jacoby photo), 88, 103, 105, 110, 121 (Horton pastel), 128, Minnesota Historical Society; p. 26, Anthony D. Hughes (Anthony D. Hughes painting); p. 37, Herkimer County (New York) Historical Society; p. 74, Norton and Peel; p. 80, Robert Jacobson; p. 147, Evelyn Burke, *Minnetonka Sun*; pp. 162, 163, 166, 167, 168, Library of Congress; p. 169, Frank W. Schlegel collection; p. 170, Baltimore Streetcar Museum, Inc.

"The Song of the Trolley" by Roy L. McCardell appeared in *Trolley Car Treasury* © 1956 by Frank Rowsome, Jr. and Stephen D. Maguire. Used by permission.

Appendixes by Jon Jackoway

Copyright © 1978 by Goodrich Lowry
Published 1979 by Lerner Publications Company

Library of Congress Cataloging Data

Lowry, Goodrich.
    Streetcar man: Tom Lowry and the Twin City Rapid Transit Company.

    Bibliography: p. 171
    Includes index.
    1. Lowry, Thomas, 1843-1909. 2. Twin City Rapid Transit Company—History. 3. Street railroads—Employees—Biography. I. Title.
HE2754.L63L68   1979   338.4'6'0924   [B]   79-2584
ISBN 0-8225-0764-1

Manufactured in the United States of America

Contents

81-97 4

Illustrations

Maps

Foreword

My grandfather died before i was born, but i was always aware of his presence. His statue was standing on Lowry Hill, and his name was often spoken.

Shortly before my mother died, she started to write her reminiscences of my grandfather, but, unhappily, she lived only long enough to make a bare beginning. Here are some of her words: "He had a great sense of humor, much courage and great charm. He had a great admiration for Lincoln and was almost as effective a storyteller. He had a great faith in the future of his city and an unswerving belief in his fellow man. The only demand he ever made on his children was—'Always look out for the underdog.' These were his last conscious words to his daughter before he died."

As I've come to know my grandfather better through a variety of sources, I've come to believe that his story, entwined as it is with the development of Minneapolis, should be told. I only wish that it could have been written by someone who knew him in the flesh, because then these pages would have glowed with the warmth which was so much a part of his nature.

G.L.

Thank You

TOM LOWRY WAS NO SAVER OF STRING OR, FOR THAT MATTER, anything else. With the exception of his *Personal Reminiscences of Abraham Lincoln*, he left behind almost nothing in the way of letters, papers, or records to enlighten a biographer. But his personality and sense of humor left their own records, which still live in the minds of others.

When I began collecting material for this book, Barbara Flanagan was kind enough to devote one of her *Minneapolis Star* columns to the life of Tom Lowry and to a request for personal recollections. As a result I received an amazing number of letters and phone calls from people who had a Tom Lowry story to tell and who contributed a lot to my understanding of a man who died 70 years ago.

My richest single source of information has been the Minneapolis History Collection of the Minneapolis Public Library. Here can be found all of the standard histories of Minneapolis, including those by Isaac Atwater, Horace B. Hudson, Marion D. Shutter, and Edward D. Neill; early tomes such as Andreas' Minnesota atlas of 1874 and maps and plat books going back to 1884; city directories dating from 1870; many hundreds of photographs, including the famed Bromley collection; almost every book ever written about early Minneapolis, ranging from *Pioneer Harvest* by Marion Cross to the *Autobiography of William Henry Eustis;* and countless files containing news items on just about every relevant subject. Dorothy

Burke, who maintains and presides over this treasury, even finds the time to exercise her unique talent for encouraging novice historians.

The Minnesota Historical Society is another priceless source of information. Russell Fridley, one of the nation's most respected historians, and Lucille Kane, who authored the valuable book *The Waterfall That Built a City,* have developed a vast collection of Minnesota historical material whose value is limited only by the time needed to explore it.

A more specialized collection is maintained by the Hennepin County Historical Society, whose chief curator, the imaginative Ruth Thorftenson, knows her way through every thicket of the county's history.

The American Association for State and Local History in Nashville, Tennessee, publishes the *Directory of Historical Societies and Agencies in the United States and Canada.* This directory led me to such friendly, helpful people as Mrs. Dwight Howell and Mr. Ralph Malcolmson in Rushville and Pleasant View, Illinois; Mrs. Philip Haring in Galesburg, Illinois; and Mrs. Jane Spellman in Ilion, New York.

The records in the Hennepin County Courthouse are intriguing sources of information. A copy of every real estate deed ever executed in Hennepin County can be found in the tract index of the register of deeds office, where the history and value of every parcel of land can be traced back to its original sale by the United States. The clerk of the probate court maintains a file on the nature and disposition of every estate probated within the county. And the clerk of the district court keeps the record of the thousands of lawsuits which have been tried within its jurisdiction. For example, the file on the 1884 suit of William S. King v. Philo Remington contains thousands of pages of testimony, including much original material on the early history of the streetcar company.

The Twin City Rapid Transit Company has published two histories of its development. The first took the form of a series of newspaper advertisements published in 1909 and is available in the Minneapolis History Collection, as is *Transit and the Twins* by Stephen A. Kieffer (1958). The Minnesota Historical Society has Frank Trumbull's technical reports on the physical condition of the Twin City Lines immediately after electrification, also published by the company.

The most comprehensive and authoritative information on our streetcar history has been assembled by the Minnesota Transportation Museum. Included in its collection are the original minutes of the Minneapolis Street Railway Company and the St. Paul City Railway Company. In 1976 the museum published Russell L. Olson's *The Electric Railways of Minnesota,* a profusely illustrated volume containing just about all the known facts on the development of streetcars in Minneapolis, St. Paul, and other Minnesota communities. The museum has also restored an original Minneapolis streetcar, which it operates on a mile of track rebuilt and electrified at Lake Harriet. George Isaacs, the museum's president, can even explain how it works.

For additional background, I benefited from Henry Villard's autobiography; *Jacob H. Schiff—His Life and Letters* by Cyrus Adler; *Men and Volts—A History of General Electric* by John Winthrop Hammond; Theodore Dreiser's *The Titan;* and *Trolley Car Treasury* by Frank Rowsome. Early editions of the *Commercial and Financial Chronicle* helped in reconstructing the early financial history of the Twin City Rapid Transit Company.

Some of the descendants of the early Boston stockholders responded most cordially to my inquiries. Charles Francis Adams was particularly helpful in referring me to Albro Martin, author of the splendid *James J. Hill and the Opening of the Northwest* and editor of the *Harvard Business History Review.* Mr. Martin introduced me to Robert Lovett, curator of manuscripts in the Baker Library of Harvard University, and Mr. Lovett unearthed a wealth of relevant correspondence between Tom Lowry, Charles Fairchild, and Henry Lee Higginson.

For an understanding of the social customs and niceties of the 1890s, the *Dual City Blue Book,* published by R. L. Polk and Company, proved most helpful, as was Mrs. E. J. Phelps, custodian of the original minutes of the Hostesses.

My most frequently used and reliable sources of information were the newspapers which have been so well preserved by the Minneapolis Public Library and the Minnesota Historical Society. The early editions of the *Minneapolis Tribune, Journal,* and *Times* and the *St. Paul Pioneer Press* and *Dispatch* offer the entire history of the Twin Cities with an impressive completeness.

Finally, I wish to express my gratitude to the two women who have gotten this book finished. My former secretary, Bernice Klask, is the only person in the world who can read my handwriting. And my wife, Louisa, is the only person in the world who can read me.

STREETCAR MAN

For Kate Stuart Lowry,
who wanted to write this book

Growing Up in Lincoln Country

THE VILLAGE OF PLEASANT VIEW IS APTLY NAMED. IT LOOKS OUT over wooded hills and down to the Illinois River three miles to the south. Springfield, the capital of Illinois, lies 50 miles to the east. To the north a country road runs through a series of small farms, the first of which was once known as the Lowry place. Pleasant View contains about 20 elderly frame homes with about 100 inhabitants; it is nearly the same size it was when Tom Lowry was growing up there more than 100 years ago.

Pleasant View and its rolling countryside may have reminded Tom's father, Sam Lowry, of Londonderry and the green hills of Ireland, where he had been raised. Moving slowly westward with the tide of migration, Sam Lowry arrived in Pleasant View in 1845 with his wife, Rachel, whom he had met in Pennsylvania, and two sons, who had been born on a small farm a little farther east. When he bought his 75-acre farm on the north edge of Pleasant View for $900, Sam was 32 years old; Rachel was 19; William was 3; and Tommy was 2.

Sam built a frame house which had two upstairs bedrooms and farmed the land which would feed and clothe his family. In those days, a large majority of the population depended directly on the land for most necessities. Sam Lowry probably grew every sort of crop and raised every kind of domestic animal. He even had a peach orchard just south of his house. In 1850 the census taker estimated the value of the farm at $3,500.

3

School was held in a log cabin, as was the Methodist Sunday school. Tom Lowry was listed as a regular attender in an old Sunday school record of the church. One can only guess what he learned in school and Sunday school, but there was another influence whose dramatic impact on his life was more certain.

Like most landowners, Sam Lowry occasionally needed a lawyer. His lawyer, as early as 1850, was Abraham Lincoln. When he visited Lincoln's Springfield office, he took Tommy with him, and when he drove a farm wagon 80 miles to Galesburg to attend the Lincoln-Douglas debate of October 7, 1858, Tommy, then 15, went too. It may have been at this time that Lincoln became an idol who was to influence strongly the direction of Tom Lowry's life.

Lombard University (later absorbed by Knox College) had recently been established at Galesburg, and its student body was a conspicuous part of the audience at the Lincoln-Douglas debate. Lombard was the second university in the country to treat men and women as equals, and Lincoln was welcomed in Galesburg with a fine banner which had been sewn by the women of Lombard. Perhaps it was this visit which aroused Tom Lowry's interest in Lombard; he enrolled there as a student three years later.

Like most universities of that day, Lombard was church-oriented. Its faculty consisted largely of Universalist clergymen; the students attended services both morning and evening each day and studied mundane subjects in between religion classes. Levity was not encouraged. The Lombard catalogues stated, "No student shall attend any dancing or other frivolous parties during term time without permission from the faculty." And under "General Conduct" appeared, "Students will not be permitted to play cards, billiards or other games leading to habits of idleness or dissipation, or to use any profane or unbecoming language." Special permission was required for young gentlemen and ladies to take walks or rides together. The university's policy on alcohol and tobacco must have been too obvious to warrant mention in the catalogues. Tuition for the regular collegiate course was $8.25 per quarter, and board

Springfield, August. 17. 1850

Mr. S. R. Lowry.

Dear Sir:

Your letter of the 13th was received a day or two ago, and I now proceed to answer it— Your first question is "What is lacking to perfect a title on the part of the defendants?" Answer— The defendants, so far as I know, do not claim to have any title, except a tax-title; and this, the court has decided to be insufficient; and I know nothing the defendants can do to perfect this title— I do not know what you mean by "the conveyances sent by mail"— The deed purporting to be made some years ago, at St. Louis, by Page (the Patentee) to Ryan, we had at the trial, and still have— That deed, in the hands of these defendants, was sought to be used as evidence of what the lawyers call an outstanding title— that is, a title owned by neither plaintiff nor defendants— The trouble with this deed was, that the plaintiff proved it to be a forgery; and I see no way in which the defendants can ever succeed unless they can somehow prove that this deed is not a forgery— This is the whole story— The case can not be gained by much talking—

A new trial was allowed upon the payment of costs; and, until the costs are paid, the defendants are liable ~~at any~~ ~~for amount~~ to be put out of possession at any moment the plaintiff may see fit to order out a writ; which, however he has not yet done— The amount of the cost is $35-83 cents, as the clerk informs me—

Yours &c
A. Lincoln—

ranged from $1.75 to $2.00 per week; so for a nine-month year, bills would have come to about $100. The cost of attending Lombard seems reasonable today, but for a farmer in the mid-nineteenth century, such as Tom Lowry's father, the cost probably made quite a dent in the family budget.

After spending two years at Lombard, Tom Lowry left due to an illness suspected of being tuberculosis. During extensive travels in the West, he recovered his health, and he may have visited Minneapolis. Returning to Pleasant View, he tried to adapt himself to life on the farm.

Ralph Malcolmson, who lives on the old Lowry place today, tells a story which he heard from his grandfather:

> One day Tom Lowry was following a horse and plow down the far side of that field over there, and all of a sudden he whoaed the horse and he sat down with his chin in his hands and he just sat there looking at the ground. His daddy walked across the field and he came up to him and he said: "Tommy, what's the matter?" And Tommy said: "Daddy, I don't want to be a farmer." And his daddy said: "Well, Tommy, what do you want to be?" And Tommy said: "I want to be a lawyer." So his daddy said: "All right, Tommy, unhitch that horse, and we'll go in town and see what we can do about it."

"Town" meant Rushville, the county seat, four miles west of Pleasant View. There Tom Lowry "read law" for two years in the office of Judge John C. Bagby. Admitted to the Illinois Bar, he took off for the infant town of Minneapolis armed only with his "law degree" and a recommendation from Bagby.

By this time, at 24, Tom Lowry bore a striking resemblance to his hero. He stood six feet two inches, and his lean, athletic frame, angular face, and humorous mouth and eyes conveyed the same humanity and sympathy which drew people so readily to Lincoln. And in addition to choosing Lincoln's vocation, he seemed to have adopted his easy manner, wit, and philosophy. At the Galesburg debate, he heard Lincoln tell a story which was apt enough to make his point and funny enough to win over his audience. Fifty years later, in his *Reminiscences of Abraham Lincoln,* Lowry wrote:

> I remember a story that Lincoln told at that meeting which is not reported in the joint debate. He said that when Douglas was in the south, he was a Southerner and, in the north, he was a Northern man. Illustrative of this, he told a story of a Yankee who had a pony that was very lazy. He secured a pair of large spurs, which had a good effect for a time, but as the pony got used to them, instead of starting up fresh with each prod, he would stick out one forefoot and lie down in the road. One day, in riding along the highway, a traveler with a fine horse overtook him. After a little, the Yankee bartered with him to trade horses. The man at first took it as an insult, but the Yankee persisted in telling him the good qualities of his pony. About that time, they were passing a clump of bushes and the Yankee saw some pheasants. He stuck his spur into the pony, who put out his forefoot and lay down. The Yankee called out: "Hold on, stranger, pheasants around here. This pony is a hunter and setter. You go on the other side of the bushes and 'skeer' up the birds and I'll shoot 'em as they come out." The stranger complied and the Yankee shot a couple of pheasants. It so impressed the man that he finally traded for the pony and paid the Yankee some "boot." They changed saddles and it happened the stranger wore spurs. The Yankee held back his horse until they came to a small stream which they had to ford. Fearing trouble, he let his horse go ahead. The traveler in midstream put his spur to the pony, who put out his foot and lay down in the middle of the stream. The Yankee called back and said: "Don't be discouraged, stranger, he's just as good for fish as he is for fowl."

Tom Lowry became a master of the apt story. Throughout his life, he found himself amid groups of men who roared with laughter at his stories and somehow came to agree with his point of view. "Tom Lowry stories" are still in circulation—60-odd years after his death. So is the legend of the man who reminded so many of Lincoln.

Early Days in Minneapolis

TOM LOWRY CAME TO MINNEAPOLIS IN 1867 AT AGE 24. MINNEAPOLIS and Lowry were destined to grow up together and, in the process, to become close friends.

When Lowry arrived, the oldest house in town had been standing for only 16 years, and there were few comforts in this booming frontier settlement of 10,000 pioneers. The streets were tracks of ungraded dirt which was often transformed into deep mud; there were no sidewalks nor utilities of any sort, except outhouses and private cisterns which stored rainwater. Practically all of the buildings were made of unpainted boards produced by the town's many sawmills. But Minneapolis' surging vitality made up for its lack of refinement.

The ending of the Civil War in 1865 had marked the beginning of the real tide of immigration into Minnesota. Civil War veterans received bonuses in the form of public land, and many looked toward the rich farming territory west of the Mississippi. Railroad construction attracted laborers from Europe to lay tracks and then settle down to farm the adjacent acreage. The water power of St. Anthony Falls attracted the men who were sawing the pine forests into boards that built the new farms and towns and the men who milled the wheat being harvested along the right-of-ways of the new railroads.

Tom Lowry was part of this migration. Evelyn Burke, in a 1944 article in *Northwestern Life* magazine, describes his arrival:

Short on cash but long on ambition, he headed for Mrs. Wilbur's boarding house where he had been directed by an eastern friend. Now, Mrs. Wilbur's was no ordinary boarding house. To the eligible young men who flocked here from the east to make their fortunes, it was a club, and to the belles of the day, it was the debutantes' delight—a steady source of cotillion partners. When gangling Tom Lowry made his appearance in a shabby worsted suit and a high plug hat, as Mrs. Wilbur's album recalled years later, it brought forth a gale of laughter from the gay young blades in the parlor. But derision soon changed to genuine admiration, and in a couple of days, the tall, skinny boarder was the life of the boarding house. His stay was short-lived, however. A few weeks later, he came into the parlor, carpet-bag in hand. "I hate to leave," he told the boys, "but I just can't stand this $8.00 a week."

Lowry's first friend in Minneapolis was probably Dr. Hannibal H. Kimball, who was also 24 years old in 1867. According to Kim-

The suspension bridge young Tom Lowry crossed upon arriving in Minneapolis

The Ferrant Building, where Tom Lowry lived for a time with Dr. Hannibal H. Kimball

ball's reminiscences, he happened to meet Lowry in Chicago when they were both headed for Minneapolis. The *Minneapolis Journal* of October 16, 1927, relates: "Boarding a train, they rode to Prairie Du Chien, Wis., where they caught the first boat headed for Minnesota. Landing in St. Paul, and walking with luggage in hand, they spent the night at the Half Way House, midway between St. Paul and St. Anthony. Arriving at the suspension bridge, the young physician and the newly graduated attorney regretfully deposited their eight-cent toll and tramped across to the infant city of Minneapolis."

Dr. Kimball rented an office on the second floor of the Ferrant Building, a two-story frame structure on the northeast corner of Nicollet Avenue and Second Street. With a frontage of 30 feet on Nicollet, the Ferrant Building had a second floor that boasted five windows, of which Dr. Kimball's quarters probably had two. This section of town was known as Bridge Square because it adjoined the suspension bridge linking Minneapolis with St. Anthony on the eastern bank of the Mississippi River. (Originally a separate city, St. Anthony merged with Minneapolis in 1872.) A few years later, a new city hall was to be built across the street from the Ferrant Building, but, in 1867, this site was a wallow for pigs and ducks.

When Lowry became dismayed by the cost of Mrs. Wilbur's, Kimball asked him to share his quarters in the Ferrant Building, and the resulting arrangement included not only office space but sleeping room as well. Lowry is credited with hammering together the crude framework of a double bed, buying a load of corn husks, and inducing a seamstress to make the rough mattress on which the young friends slept. Lowry agreed to pay half of the six dollars which was Kimball's monthly rent.

It soon became apparent that it was awkward to conduct a medical examination and a legal conference in the same room at the same time. A partition provided two offices, and the bed was probably kept in an area behind the offices. Since the Ferrant Building was 120 feet deep, there was plenty of room.

Dr. Kimball owned a stylish cutaway coat and a silk hat, and, since the two friends were of a similar build, they used to flip a coin to determine which one would wear them to a social function at the Nicollet House and which one would stay home. They also shared a riding horse, which was pastured on Fourth Street, and depended equally on a buffalo robe to keep the bed warm in winter. When the doctor was called out at night, he took the robe with him in the sleigh, with attendant hardship on Lowry. Their meals were provided by Russell Munger, Minneapolis' first police chief, at $1.50 per week, probably just what they could afford. Doctors' fees were generally 50 cents a visit, and lawyers' fees were commensurate. Clients and patients doubtless were scarce during that first year.

During these early days, Tom Lowry formed another friendship which was equally close and would last even longer. Clinton Morrison, at 25, was about the same age as the young roommates, but, unlike them, he had come to town with his family 12 years earlier and was firmly established in the hierarchy of the young community. His father, Dorilus Morrison, had learned the lumber business in Bangor, Maine, and, with capital in hand, had come to St. Anthony with his family in 1855. Starting with a logging operation on the Rum River, he soon built a sawmill at the falls and later became a dominant force in the Minneapolis Mill Company, which controlled all of the water power on the west bank of the river. When Minneapolis was incorporated early in 1867, Dorilus Morrison was elected its first mayor. His residence, the spacious Villa Rosa, where the Minneapolis Institute of Arts stands today, was the social center of the city.

While Lowry was gregarious, witty, speculative, and sometimes hilarious, Clinton Morrison was the opposite. In the *History of the City of Minneapolis, Minnesota,* edited by Isaac Atwater, one biographer wrote, "Mr. Morrison is of a particularly reticent disposition. He has his chosen friends who are warmly attached to him but does not readily assimilate with ephemeral attachments." Their friendship must have been a good example of the attraction of opposites, because the jovial Irishman and the dour Yankee became the closest of friends and business associates. It is also clear that Clinton's father, the prestigious Dorilus, adopted Tom Lowry as a protégé and gave him the considerable advantage of his support.

An early Minneapolis businessman, Lac Stafford, told this story in an interview in the *Minneapolis Journal* of August 18, 1915:

> Mr. Stafford spoke of Clinton Morrison. He was one of Mr. Lowry's closest friends, and Dorilus Morrison, father of Clinton, had a world of confidence in young Tom Lowry. In fact, it is related to this day that many a time when things were so tight that no one else would come to the rescue, Dorilus Morrison backed his faith in young Tom Lowry. Mr. Stafford has a story about this.
>
> "Dorilus Morrison was sitting by his fireside one night when his son, Clinton, came in and took the chair across the hearth," said Mr. Stafford.
>
> " 'Father,' said Clinton, 'they tell me that Tom Lowry is in a pretty bad fix.'

" 'Oh, I guess not,' responded the first Mayor of Minneapolis.

" 'Yes, he is,' responded the son, 'they say there is no saving him this time.'

" 'I've helped young Lowry before,' commented the father.

" 'I know,' responded the son, 'but they say he is so tight up against it that even you can't save him this time.'

"Whereupon the battle light showed in the eyes of Dorilus Morrison and he sent for young Lowry posthaste and, with his own good cash, showed those talkative people that Dorilus Morrison *could* save young Lowry no matter how tight the pinch. It was a little game that Clinton and Tom had fixed up between them."

An 1867 picture of Tom Lowry and his friend Clinton Morrison shows Lowry lounging in a velvet-collared cutaway and high silk hat (probably the property of Dr. Kimball), and Morrison standing similarly clad but with the expression of a minister. For a boy from the country, Lowry was off to a flying start.

Dorilus Morrison, the first mayor of Minneapolis. He enjoyed coming to Tom Lowry's rescue "no matter how tight the pinch."

Tom Lowry *(left)* and Clinton Morrison, son of Dorilus Morrison

Real Estate: The Real Action

In the spring of 1868, after less than a year in the Ferrant Building, Lowry and Kimball bought the lease, the practice, and the office contents of Dr. A. E. Ames in the Harrison Block. The purchase price was $60, which they borrowed from Clinton Morrison. One of the town's best addresses, the Harrison Block was a bleak three-story gray stone building erected in 1863 on the northeast corner of Washington and Nicollet. When the young men moved, the bed went with them, and the first arrangement of their Harrison Block office may have been much like what they had in the Ferrant Building, buffalo robe and all. There was still no water or gas in downtown Minneapolis, and wood stoves furnished the heat.

Within a year, Lowry and Kimball separated to form partnerships of a more professional nature. Lowry joined lawyer Austin H. Young, who was 12 years older and who had also grown up on an Illinois farm. The Young and Lowry partnership continued until 1872, when Young was appointed judge of the newly formed court of common pleas. Kimball went into practice with Dr. Calvin Gibson Goodrich, who was to play an important part in Tom Lowry's life. Dr. Goodrich moved into the old Ames office with Kimball, while Lowry probably moved into Young's office, which was in the same building. The fate of the bed is unrecorded.

Dr. Goodrich had grown up on a farm near Winchester, Indiana, and early in life had worked for his brother, who was county

**Dr. Calvin Gibson Goodrich,
Tom Lowry's father-in-law,
played an important part in
Lowry's life.**

surveyor. He became proficient in "handling the chain, the axe,
and the transit," and though he turned to medicine, he never lost
his keen interest in real estate. After obtaining a medical degree in
Cincinnati, he moved to nearby Oxford, Ohio, where he built a
prosperous practice. Coming to Minneapolis in 1868, at age 48, he
settled his wife, two sons, and two daughters in an elegant $20,000
home at Seventh Street and Fourth Avenue South, where Charlie's
Cafe now stands. During his years in Oxford, Dr. Goodrich was
said to have been active in the Underground Railroad, and his
household included a few liberated slaves, who may have been
Minneapolis' first black settlers. Three years before his move, he
had bought a 148-acre farm for $5,180, or $35 per acre, on what
was later known as Lowry Hill.

  Dr. Goodrich was a man of capital, which, along with his medical skills, soon made him one of the town's prominent citizens. He
was short and stocky, and although his appearance was dignified,
his eyes harbored a friendly, mischievous twinkle.

  As partners of Goodrich and Young, the former roommates had
secured a foothold in the town's establishment. But Lowry's interest in law was soon to be combined with a still keener interest in
the fascinating game of real estate. Isaac Atwater, who was also a

lawyer, wrote in his history of Minneapolis: "The practice of law at that period in this part of the country, was meager. It consisted chiefly of land cases, and its forum was more in the land office than in the courts. It furnished little occupation to satisfy an eager and ambitious temper." As in most frontier communities, the real action was in real estate.

In Minneapolis today, accumulations of money are usually invested in stocks and bonds. But in the Minneapolis of 1868, any excess cash that could be earned, begged, or borrowed was likely to go into the purchase of real estate. The securities of that day were both scarce and distrusted, but the real estate of a growing community was a much-coveted possession.

Soon after his arrival in Minneapolis, Lowry's name began to appear on documents in the register of deeds office as witness and notary public, or, in other words, as the lawyer in the deal. But it was not until November 21, 1868, that his name began to appear as a buyer. On that date he purchased from one Ovid Pinney, for $300, Lot 9, Block 168, Town of Minneapolis. This lot was located in the vicinity of Seven Corners, where Washington Avenue meets Cedar—not a fashionable neighborhood, but a good place for a workingman to build a solid frame house.

Lumber was cheap in Minneapolis; utilities consisted of cisterns that held the rainwater. If a man wanted to build it himself, he could have a good home, including an outhouse, for $500 plus the cost of the lot. When Thomas Lowry purchased his first lot, he had no intention of building a house at Seven Corners. He had simply taken his first step in the real estate business.

His second purchase was made a few days later, on December 14, 1868. Comprising a full quarter-section, or 160 acres of land, in the vicinity of Medicine Lake, the property would have a cash value today of more than $10,000 an acre, or about $1,600,000. But Lowry paid $100.

His next deal, in February 1869, brought him five lots in the Seven Corners area at a wholesale rate of $120 per lot. He prompt-

ly resold one for $350 and chalked up his first profit. But, as part of
the deal, he bought another quarter-section of land in the vicinity of
present-day Hopkins. At $1,300, or about $8 per acre, this tract
must have been a relatively choice piece of outlying property.

During the balance of 1869, Lowry bought two lots near Seven
Corners for $800 and sold them for $1,400; he bought 40 acres
near Hopkins for $1,000 and sold them for $1,300; and he bought a
small house for $1,067 and sold it for $1,000—perhaps the roof
leaked. By the end of 1869, Lowry had realized profits of $1,063.
He had on hand sundry pieces of real estate which had cost him
$2,204, much of which was probably borrowed from friends and
relatives in Illinois.

As the following year began, Lowry continued to make real estate transactions in much the same fashion. The four remaining
$120 lots were sold to Dr. Goodrich for $1,000, bringing a handsome profit of $520. Several additional lots were purchased in var-
ious parts of town. And then the pattern changed. On April 30,
1870, Thomas Lowry bought the home of Benning and Margaret
Haney on Second Street North between Fifth and Sixth Avenues
for $5,000, of which $1,500 was cash. Just inside the city limits
and only two blocks from the pasturelands of Bassett's Creek, the
Haney house enjoyed a pleasant, residential location. With a value
of $5,000, it must have been one of the town's nicer homes.

Shortly after purchasing the Haney house, Lowry began to liq-
uidate his real estate inventory; several of the sales were made to
Dr. Goodrich. One of the pieces which Dr. Goodrich purchased
was the first lot Lowry had owned—the one which he had bought
from Ovid Pinney. But the deed conveying it to Dr. Goodrich,
dated July 11, 1870, was signed not only by Thomas Lowry but
also by Harriet Lowry—his wife.

On July 20, 1870, Lowry sold the Haney house to a real estate
dealer for what he had paid, $5,000. The deed was signed by
Thomas Lowry as a single man. Had this house been bought for a
home? Had he carried Harriet over the threshold? If there was a

marriage, there is no record of it in Hennepin County.

Just five months later, on the evening of December 14, 1870, the best carriages in town were drawn up in front of Dr. Goodrich's residence for what the *Tribune* called the most brilliant social event of the year. The invitations, engraved for the first time in Minneapolis history, had summoned the doctor's many friends to the marriage ceremony of his 16-year-old daughter, Beatrice, to Thomas Lowry.

Who was Harriet? Her identity may never be known, but there was an interesting comment some 50 years later. In 1920, the *Tribune,* in a souvenir issue, reran its account of the marriage in Dr. Goodrich's home, including the statement that Clinton Morrison had served as best man. This story brought a protest from Dr. H. H. Kimball, who was still living and who insisted with great conviction that he, not Morrison, had stood up for Tom. Could there have been two marriages? Could Morrison have stood up for Tom and Beatrice, and could Kimball have stood up for Tom and Harriet? Kimball would have known. Dr. Goodrich, who received the deed with Harriet's name on it, would have known. And Beatrice probably would not.

Thomas Lowry's wife, Beatrice, enjoyed much popularity.

Developing Residential Communities

BEATRICE GOODRICH, NOW MRS. THOMAS LOWRY, WAS NOT ONLY
beautiful and talented, but also endowed with charm, and she must
have been as well liked as her popular husband. She once said that
when she was a child, her father, Dr. Goodrich, used to put her to
bed with the words "Trice, I want you to smile and to smile all the
time. You were put on this earth to make people happy and the
best way to make people happy is to smile at them." She undoubtedly made her husband happy, and, as a counterweight to his more
adventurous instincts, she probably contributed more than her
share to the successful life they enjoyed.

Shortly after the marriage, Lowry bought a home, again for
$5,000, on Seventh Street near Third Avenue, about a block from
the Goodrich home. While his law practice was growing, he found
the real estate business more exciting and more profitable. And he
now had an additional reason for making money—a wife.

* * *

Minneapolis is known today as a city of people who own their
own homes. Even in the city's early years, this was true. Andreas'
1874 Minnesota atlas comments:

> In building every advantage is offered. The owners of proper-
> ty are unusually liberal, and will exert themselves to the ut-
> most to encourage the settlement of the city, by selling their

> lots at very moderate prices and giving the very easiest terms.
> Of course lumber is very cheap, and everything in the con-
> struction of a building being manufactured here, they can be
> procured from first hands at low rates. It really does seem that
> nothing is wanting to satisfy a person seeking a home.

The atlas goes on to speak in general of the many residential
communities, and in particular of two:

> The beautiful Groveland Addition is rapidly becoming a most
> charming village in itself. The wide Hennepin Avenue, which
> passes through it, is firmly-macadamized, and the spacious
> lots are fertile and prolific. Those seeking delightful residence
> property should view this favored spot. Another addition of
> somewhat different character is the South Side Addition. Here
> are located the extensive Harvester Works and a Bedstead fac-
> tory and other manufacturing establishments will soon be
> built. Already 375 lots in this addition have been purchased,
> and many improved by the mechanics who find employment
> in this district.

Both the Groveland Addition and the South Side Addition were
the handiwork of Thomas Lowry. But his first effort was of a hum-
bler sort, and it was this earlier subdivision which bore his name.

Lowry's Addition consisted of 6⅔ acres of land lying south of
Franklin Avenue between Park and Portland. After purchasing
this tract from Robert B. Langdon in February 1872, for $800 in
cash plus a mortgage of $8,500, Lowry platted it as Block 1 and
Block 2, each block containing 16 lots with dimensions of 50 feet on
the street by 130 feet in depth. Immediately after platting, he sold
Block 2 to lawyer Albee Smith for $500 cash plus a mortgage of
$8,000.

The lots in Block 1 moved slowly. Dr. Goodrich bought four lots
in March for $400 per lot, but this was the end of the action until a
year and a half later, when three lots were sold for a total of
$2,050. The remaining nine lots were finally sold to another dealer
in October 1875, for $8,100. Adding the proceeds of the lots in
Block 1 to the sale price of Block 2, one might think that, with sales

of $20,250 versus a purchase price of $9,300, Lowry's Addition was quite a success.

But the real estate business in the seventies was not that simple. Almost every transaction involved taking a mortgage from the purchaser and obtaining a release of the property from the mortgage already on it. Often the release was obtained by making a small cash payment and assigning the new mortgage to the holder of the old one. The process was frequently interrupted by default, foreclosure, sheriff's sale, and a pile of legal documents a foot high. Each of the 32 lots in Lowry's Addition has a fairly turbulent early legal history. Much of this confusion was still going on during the years when Lowry was engaged in larger and more complex deals, which bred their own mountains of complications.

The Groveland Addition was a considerably more ambitious enterprise. It covered about 220 acres divided into 75 blocks, much more area than the 6 acres and 2 blocks of Lowry's Addition. Ranging over pleasant, rolling countryside, this subdivision extended from Lyndale Avenue to Fremont and from Franklin north to the Great Northern Railway tracks. It consisted largely of part of the 148-acre farm which Dr. Goodrich had purchased before his move to Minneapolis. On October 14, 1872, he sold a one-half interest in the farm to his son-in-law, Thomas Lowry, for $42,000, or $570 per acre, which is what the property was probably worth. At the same time Lowry and his partners, the Herrick Brothers, a prominent real estate firm, bought interests in the 100-acre tract lying directly north of the Goodrich farm, at prices ranging from $500 to $800 per acre. On October 16, 1872, this northerly tract, together with 120 acres from the Goodrich farm, was platted as the Groveland Addition. The northerly tract, being closer to downtown, was the first to develop. Almost all of the original structures, which were mostly commercial buildings and apartments, are long gone. The area today contains Parade Stadium, Dunwoody Institute, and Interstate 94. But in 1872, it was laid out as 30 blocks that were highly regarded by the real estate trade. The sale of this property was, in fact, the medium through which the prestigious Academy of Music was purchased by Lowry and his partners.

The Academy of Music was built in 1871 by Joseph Hodges of Providence, Rhode Island. Located on the southwest corner of Washington and Hennepin and patterned after the Academy of Music in New York, it was by far the most elegant Minneapolis building of its day. And, for more than 10 years, it was the center of the city's commercial and cultural life.

Hodges bought the land, 9,040 square feet measuring 80 feet on Washington by 113 feet on Hennepin, for $17,000, or about $2 per square foot. Only 15 years earlier, this property had been acquired from the United States government as a part of the Stevens Claim for $1.25 an acre. The site that cost Hodges $17,000 totaled about one-fifth of an acre, which meant that its original purchase price was approximately 26 cents. (It's a small wonder that speculators were intrigued by the possibilities of frontier real estate.) Hodges invested an additional $100,000 in the four-story building. He bor-

This painting depicts the Academy of Music, where Lowry had an office on the second floor.

rowed $50,000 of that sum from Dorilus Morrison, who took a first mortgage on the property.

The two top floors, under a handsome mansard slate roof, contained a splendid auditorium with a balcony running around three sides and seats for 1,300 people. The second floor was the prestige address for the professional men of Minneapolis, while the ground floor housed the Metropolitan National Bank and the city's better clothing stores. In a spacious cellar, Central Hall, 100 feet by 39 feet, housed the numerous festivals and dances for which, according to the _Tribune,_ Minneapolis was "famed."

The auditorium and Central Hall were served by three Claggstone steam boilers powering the city's first low-pressure steam heating system. Since the building was equipped with eight chimneys, the offices and stores were probably heated by stoves, which burned the waste slabs and sides from the sawmills.

In February 1873, about a year after the completion of the building, Hodges sold the Academy to a syndicate made up of Thomas Lowry (40 percent), the Herrick Brothers (40 percent), and Dr. Goodrich (20 percent). The sale price of $117,000 plus assumption of the $50,000 mortgage might appear to have yielded Hodges a profit of $50,000 over his cost. But since payment was made in other Minneapolis real estate, rather than cash, the actual profit is hard to determine. Among the properties which Hodges received in payment for the Academy were 9 of the 30 blocks in the northerly portion of the Groveland Addition for a price of $75,000 and Tom Lowry's $5,000 home for $16,500. This was probably Beatrice's first experience in suddenly becoming involved in a real estate deal.

Tom Lowry, Dr. Goodrich, and the Herrick Brothers moved their offices to the Academy's second floor; they were now both owners and occupants of the city's foremost building. As for Hodges, he was declared bankrupt about a year after his sale of the Academy. By that time, he had disposed of Lowry's house and one-third of the Groveland property, but the remainder was, as part of the bankruptcy proceedings, sold back to Lowry for $500 plus the obligation to pay an $18,000 mortgage, all of which makes it even more difficult to distinguish between the winners and the losers. In any event, the Academy of Music served Lowry as an office address of distinction until it burned to the ground on Christmas Day, 1884.

The development of the South Side Addition was a very different type of enterprise. On January 1, 1874, the *Tribune* carried as a news story the following message: "The Directors of Minneapolis Harvester Company at their last meeting decided to put 120 or more men at work building the Hubbard Reaping and Mowing Machines on or before February 1. This, together with other large manufactories about to be erected in this vicinity, makes a large advance in the price of lots in the South Side Addition certain. Call on Thomas Lowry, Room 1, Academy of Music, at once before the prices are raised." On the next day, following this fortuitous piece of advance publicity, Lowry's paid advertisements began to make their daily appearances on the *Tribune*'s front page:

SOUTH SIDE ADDITION

50 LOTS SOLD IN TWO WEEKS

GREAT BARGAINS FOR THIRTY DAYS LONGER

CALL SOON AND GET YOUR CHOICE

NO CASH PAYMENTS REQUIRED FROM

PARTIES WHO WILL BUILD—APPLY AT ONCE TO

THOMAS LOWRY, ROOM NO. 1, ACADEMY OF MUSIC

Just two months earlier, Lowry had bought from Dorilus Morrison, who also owned the Minneapolis Harvester Company, a one-half interest in a tract of 150 acres between Lake Street and Twenty-Sixth Street, and Minnehaha and Thirty-First Avenues. He paid close to $1,000 per acre, which was then a fancy price for outlying acreage. On December 8, 1873, Lowry and Morrison platted this property under the name of the South Side Addition, and the promotion was under way.

Unlike Lowry's Addition and Groveland Addition, this development was designed for sale to the men who worked in the adjoining factories, notably the Minneapolis Harvester Company, which in later years was known as the Minneapolis Moline Plant. The lots were 48 feet wide by 152 feet deep and sold for $400 to $600, with easy terms for those agreeing to build. Most of the houses cost less than $500. There were still no utilities of any kind, unless an outhouse might be so classified. Even a well was considered an extravagance. But the houses were well built, and most of them are still there and in good repair 100 years later. The neighborhood today appears pleasant and comfortable.

During 1874 and 1875, the first two years of the development, most of the sales were made to other real estate dealers, speculators, and contractors. A purchaser could buy an entire block of 24 lots for $300 per lot; or 15 lots for $400 per lot; or 8 lots for $450 apiece; or 4 lots at a price of $500 each. If someone wanted a single lot, it would cost about $600, but a cash payment was not required.

The South Side Addition was a success. Like the Groveland Addition, it provided some cash, but, more important, it provided well-regarded lots which could be used as currency in the purchase of other real estate.

Rounding out the diversity in Lowry's early real estate holdings was a property known alternately as the Lowry Block and the North Star Building. In March 1872, Clinton Morrison and Thomas Lowry bought two lots on Washington Avenue for $17,500, and three months later, they sold the inside lot to John deLaittre for $12,500. In 1875, Lowry and Morrison built on their corner lot a handsome three-story brick building, and, since it's still there, it must have been well constructed. With dimensions of 66 feet on Washington and 82 feet on Kansas (now Second Avenue North), the entire structure, which probably cost $35,000, was leased to the North Star Boot and Shoe Company.

This fast-growing enterprise manufactured shoes and boots, which were sold both wholesale and retail. The new building housed 125 workmen, 4 office men, and 5 men in the ground floor sales room; it also contained packing and storage rooms, and head-quarters for 7 traveling salesmen. The payroll was $1,050 per week and the rent was probably $500 per month. The business was managed by Major C. B. Heffelfinger, one of the principal officers of the Minnesota First Regiment in its famous charge at the Battle of Gettysburg.

Shoes were important in the 1870s, and the *Tribune*'s description of the stylish Lowry-Goodrich wedding included the statement that "8 out of 10 guests wore shoes from Heffelfinger's." Their chief competitor was Gotzian and Hyde, who may have authored the jingle:

> If you would with God reside,
> Buy your shoes from Gotzian and Hyde.
> But if you would with the Devil linger,
> Buy your shoes from Heffelfinger.

In the same year of 1875, Lowry published an advertisement which offered a full description of the real estate which, in one way or another, he had accumulated during the five years following his marriage. The ad ran:

WANTED IMMEDIATELY

$100,000 in cash and $125,000 in mortgages in exchange for first class real estate on "hard pan" basis.

Take your choice of the following list of property and come and make an offer, but don't bid unless you want what you bid on. If you are minus the cash and mortgages, trade me lumber or something else I can use. In fact, I won't be particular if I can accommodate you and not bankrupt myself. South Side lots have *proved* a success. Last year I sold them at $400 each and some people said "too much." This year they are selling at $550 and $600 each "and not a very good year for selling." I have about two hundred more of the same sort left.

Look *carefully* over the following list and I think you can suit yourself.

There followed a detailed description of property including:

> 200 Lots in the South Side Addition and an additional 60 acres lying just to the north of it.
>
> 400 Lots in the southerly or residential portion of Groveland's Addition with the notation "on long time or any terms to suit purchasers, if requisite improvements are made."
>
> 10 Lots in the northerly or commercial portion of Groveland's Addition.
>
> 9 Lots in Lowry's Addition.
>
> A "good brick residence on Nicollet between 6 & 7 Streets."
>
> 2 small houses.
>
> 5 Lots in the vicinity of 2nd Ave., So. and 15th St.
>
> 4 Lots in the vicinity of Park Ave. & 15th St.
>
> The North Star Shoe site and two additional 66 foot lots on Washington between 2nd & 3rd Ave., No.
>
> A half block bordered by Washington, 5th Ave. No. & 3rd St. No.
>
> 20 feet of "business property on Nicollet."
>
> A "Fine Stone Building" on the corner of Washington & 12 Ave. So.
>
> A "Large Hotel" on the corner of 2nd St. & 12 Ave. So.
>
> 30 Acres between Lyndale Ave. No. and 3rd St. No. and between 26th Ave. No. and 29th Ave. No.

Following the description of the property, the advertisement concluded with this statement: "After you become the happy purchaser of a valuable piece of real estate at your own price, if anyone asks you why I sold it so cheap, you can say to them that I'm in partnership mid mine brudder, un I vants to beat him."

While Lowry had no brother to take for a partner, he held most of the properties listed in partnership with various individuals, including Dr. Goodrich, Dorilus Morrison, Clinton Morrison, and the Herrick Brothers. While the above inventory might have been worth about $500,000, Lowry's equity could not have been more than half that amount, which was further reduced by the debt with which it was encumbered.

In 1874, Lowry undertook his most personal real estate venture. Selecting seven acres of choice high ground on the corner of Hennepin and Groveland, he built a mansion which was to make the area known as Lowry Hill. The cost was said to be $40,000. This site is presently occupied by the North American Life building, the Walker Art Center, and the Guthrie Theater.

Faced with red brick and crowned by a mansard roof, the Lowry home contained most of the elegant features of an 1874 house, including a ballroom, an art gallery, a drawing room, smoking rooms, mahogany paneling, Gobelin tapestries, and Tiffany bronzes. The heating system used steam that came by pipe from the barn.

But the mansion's principal feature was a charming hostess in the person of Beatrice. Thanks to her, in the years that followed, Number 2 Groveland Terrace became known as a warm house and a happy gathering place for the people who were building Minneapolis. It also served as a perfect stage for the appearance on the scene of Colonel William S. King.

Lowry's mansion, which was built on the corner of Hennepin and Groveland, gave the area the name Lowry Hill.

Organization of the
Minneapolis Street Railway Company

COLONEL KING, WHO WAS TO PLAY AN IMPORTANT PART IN Lowry's life, was an almost unbelievable character. Only 47 in the summer of 1875, he had already survived the equivalent of three active lives. Leaving an upstate New York farm at 12, he supported himself for eight years as a teamster. Turning to politics, he became a passionate abolitionist, the 1850 equivalent of a radical. He launched a political newspaper at Cooperstown, New York, and soon thereafter, at nearby Cherry Valley, he organized a political club which may have been, in 1853, the country's first organization to bear the name *Republican*. Nearby Albany was then the national focal point of abolitionism, and King soon became intimate with the movement's leaders. His merit was recognized by his appointment as a colonel of the New York State Militia.

At age 30, in the summer of 1858, King moved to Minneapolis, bringing his title of colonel and his radical ideas. He promptly set about writing and publishing a weekly newspaper, the *State Atlas,* which was chiefly concerned with abolitionism and the sins of the Minnesota Democratic Party, which was then in power. His vitriolic pen and his overwhelming energy soon made him the driving force behind the young Republican Party in Minnesota, and when Minnesota and the nation turned to Abraham Lincoln in 1860, King became the state's undisputed Republican boss. As the Civil War began, King moved to Washington and was appointed postmaster of the House of Representatives. He held this influential position, with the exception of one two-year term, until 1873.

In addition to his other activities, the colonel had found the time and resources to assemble a notable tract of choice real estate. Named for his father, the Reverend Lyndon King, Lyndale Farm had, by 1873, reached the impressive size of 1,400 acres. Lying around the lovely lakes of Calhoun and Harriet, Lyndale Farm was a beautiful property, but it lay well outside Minneapolis' city limits and remote from its residential areas. The tract had been acquired at prices from $75 to $125 per acre and was heavily encumbered by purchase-money mortgages bearing interest at rates of 10 percent and up. The only really good solution for this sort of real estate problem would be a public transportation service linking Lyndale Farm to the bulk of the Minneapolis population. And to this solution Colonel King gave his attention.

On July 1, 1873, the Minneapolis Street Railway Company was organized by incorporators King, Dorilus Morrison (mayor and lumber mogul), W. D. Washburn (miller), R. J. Mendenhall (banker), W. P. Westfall (banker), J. C. Oswald (liquor dealer), Paris Gibson (proprietor of the North Star Woolen Mill), W. W. Eastman (lumberman), R. B. Langdon (railroad contractor), and W. W. McNair (lawyer and landowner). While there was no more prestigious group of men in town, there was very little cash in Minneapolis at the time. It was relatively easy to assemble a group of men to start almost any enterprise, but finding the required money was much more difficult.

An understanding of Colonel King's approach to this problem requires a brief detour into the history of Ilion, New York. It was there that Eliphalet Remington, working in his father's forge, made and perfected the famous breech-loaded Remington rifle. During the Civil War, the Remington Armory and the town of Ilion were greatly expanded to meet the needs of the Northern armies. The end of the war and the abruptly cancelled government contracts found the Remingtons scrambling to create a means of employing their expanded work force and factories.

The Remington enterprises had passed into the hands of Eliphalet's sons, Philo, Samuel, and Eliphalet III. Samuel went abroad and proved himself an excellent salesman of guns in the courts of the fractious rulers of Europe. The more conventional Philo, taking charge in Ilion, manufactured guns for the domestic market as well as the guns that Samuel was selling abroad. He also undertook a number of additional ventures, including the manufacture of agricultural machinery, sewing machines, and typewriters. Then, in 1871, the Frankfort and Ilion Street Railroad Company was built to link by horsecar the towns of Herkimer, Mohawk, Frankfort, and Ilion. And in 1872, the Remington Agricultural Works produced a steam streetcar and put it in service on the new railroad.

The Remingtons had not literally beaten their swords into plowshares, but they had, perhaps, done the best they could. In 1873, the Remington enterprises were on the crest. Philo was said not only to be free of debt but also to have several million dollars in his National Bank of Ilion. And the Remingtons had just gone into the streetcar business. Illion was the logical source of the cash which was so scarce in Minneapolis, particularly since Colonel King was in an ideal position to exploit this opportunity.

Ilion must have been a second home to the colonel. It was just a few miles from his former base in Cooperstown, and both King's first and second wives had been Ilion women. In fact, his first wife, Mary Elizabeth Stevens, was the sister-in-law of Eliphalet Remington III, so the colonel was, in a sense, Philo Remington's brother-in-law. As an officer of Congress during the war, he may well have had dealings with the Remingtons; in 1871 King was in Ilion, guiding Philo Remington in the acquisition of a large tract of land on Puget Sound near the projected terminus of the Northern Pacific Railroad. So the two men were doubtless good friends.

*   *   *

On August 13, 1873, one Philo Osgood "and a group of his friends" subscribed for most of the capital stock of the Minneapolis Street Railway Company. The minutes recorded the holdings:

Philo Osgood	2,490 shares
William S. King	5 shares
S. E. Neiler	5 shares
total	2,500 shares

Osgood was elected president of the company. The manager of an Ilion hotel owned by the Remingtons, Osgood was probably serving as the agent of the men who actually owned the stock. An assessment of $5 per share produced the modest sum of $12,500 as the initial capital funds of the company.

Neiler was cashier of the one-year-old Northwestern National Bank. He was elected treasurer of the company, and the bank became the company's general office and depository.

Along with the money, there arrived from Ilion a steam-powered streetcar, the fifth of its kind produced by the Remington Works. It weighed 11,000 pounds; it could run from 15 to 20 miles an hour; and, while seating only 24 passengers, it could carry 75. There was a water tank in the rear, a boiler in front, and on both ends was the label *MSRR Co. No. 1.* The streetcar was advertised as "noiseless." For several days, it made test runs on the Milwaukee and St. Paul tracks, carrying city aldermen, county commissioners, and other citizens. The price of the engine was $5,000, but the amount became academic when, after a few days, the steam car was shipped back to Ilion. Perhaps it was thought impractical to lay the heavy track the steam car required on Minneapolis "streets." Or perhaps it was concluded that "the horse is here to stay."

Soon, though, the new company started laying a very modest type of track, which probably extended a mile along Third Street from Fourth Avenue North as far as Eighth Avenue South. But there then occurred the Jay Cooke panic, one of those financial spasms which proved devastating to pioneer towns of the new West.

E. Remington & Sons,
Ilion, Herkimer County, N. Y.

Noiseless Steam Motor for Street Railways.

We call your attention to our *NOISELESS STEAM MOTOR for Street Railways, and herewith present a cut of the same, with dimensions, weight, power, and cost of operating.*

Weight for ordinary work and grades, 11,000 pounds
Increased weight when required for heavier grades and loads

An advertisement for the steam streetcars produced by the Remington Works

Jay Cooke and Company of Philadelphia had emerged from the Civil War as the outstanding banking house of America. When Cooke agreed to finance the construction of the Northern Pacific Railroad from Duluth to Puget Sound, and when Congress munificently awarded a land grant of 40 million acres, there were few who doubted that the project would succeed. But the contracting companies spent the money faster than Cooke could sell the bonds, and in the fall of 1873, both Cooke and the railroad collapsed. Minneapolis, which served as field headquarters for the enterprise, was particularly hard hit. Many hopeful young businesses, including the Minneapolis Street Railway Company, went into hibernation. The tracks were torn up before they were used, and the first chapter of the streetcar company's history came to an end.

The company's revival was an incidental detail in the unraveling of one of the periodic crises in Colonel King's personal affairs. The panic of 1873 found the colonel greatly overextended; his properties were encumbered with every conceivable type of debt. But while most men in comparable situations were quietly leaving town, King continued to exude the utmost confidence. Early in 1875, however, two of his creditors sued him and obtained sheriff's attachments to most of his real estate. These attachments, which wiped out the only remaining basis for his credit, would surely have been the straw which broke the back of most camels, but, in Colonel King's case, their only effect was to dispatch him posthaste to Ilion for a conference with his friend Philo Remington.

He told Remington that, to stand off his creditors, he needed a loan of about $150,000 (at least $1,500,000 in today's currency), and he offered to give Remington title to all of his and his wife's real and personal property as security for the loan. Remington was reluctant. Business conditions were no better in the East than in Minneapolis, and to make matters worse, some of Remington's foreign customers, having troubles of their own, were lagging in their remittances. The mighty Remington enterprises were in a definite squeeze. But Philo finally agreed to send his lawyer, Judge Amos

Prescott, and his banker, F. C. Shepherd, cashier of the Ilion National Bank, to Minneapolis to appraise King's properties.

When Prescott and Shepherd arrived in early June of 1875, they were met by King and his lawyer, Thomas Lowry. The visitors were probably taken from the train directly to Lowry's imposing mansion, which looked out over two miles of pioneer sprawl to St. Anthony Falls and the clustered mills and railroad yards of the bright new milling center. When the German butler ushered them in and took their hats, they could have thought themselves back East, were it not for the extraordinary informality of their hosts.

It was almost inevitable that Lowry should have been King's lawyer. In his autobiography, William Henry Eustis, a lawyer and a supporter of many Minneapolis projects, commented on the personalities of the two men: "Then there were King and Lowry of a more jovial disposition. Both of them had their ups and downs in the financial world and their hilarious dispositions seemed a wise provision of nature to enable them with a smile to meet their losses and reverses." Despite a difference in age (King was then 47; Lowry, 32), the two men must have been much alike; each was undoubtedly fun to be with.

But they were also very different. King was short and stocky, while Lowry had the slim, lanky, six-foot-plus frame of Abraham Lincoln. King used to boast that he never read a deed before signing it; that he never kept a book of records or accounts; and that he swept his mind completely clean of every detail of a business deal at the moment of its completion. Lowry, on the other hand, with his casual ways and scorn of formality, would often astonish his associates by the most precise grasp of some intricate detail of a complex problem. But in their optimism, joyful appreciation of life, and love of their fellow man, they were kindred spirits. Everybody liked them and they liked each other.

After several days in the company of their enthusiastic hosts, lawyer Prescott and banker Shepherd had formed a favorable impression of Minneapolis in general and of the value of Colonel

King's property in particular. On June 10, 1875, Prescott, Shepherd, and King departed for Ilion to finalize the Remington loan to King, and as Lowry happened to be going East on the same day, the four men rode the same train to Chicago. Such are the coincidences which change men's lives.

In later years, Lowry wrote, "On the train we arranged to take up the matter of building the Minneapolis Street Railway, and I agreed to meet them in Ilion, New York, a few days later to consummate the arrangement. We met in Ilion and the re-organization was perfected. It was arranged that Philo Osgood should be the President of the company and I should be the Vice President. That was my first connection with the Minneapolis Street Railway Company."

The company was again capitalized, with 2,500 shares of stock with a total par value of $250,000, subscribed as follows:

Mrs. Carrie M. King (the colonel's wife)	1,000 shares
Philo Osgood	250 shares
Amos H. Prescott	300 shares
Floyd Shepherd	500 shares
James Tuckerman	350 shares
Thomas Lowry	100 shares
total	2,500 shares

Mrs. King's stock, with the rest of the King assets, was pledged to Philo Remington, and the other stockholders, except Lowry, were Remington's associates. Philo Osgood was again elected president; Thomas Lowry was named vice-president; and James Tuckerman moved from Ilion to Minneapolis to assume the duties of general manager. A stock assessment of $20 per share provided an initial working capital of $50,000.

On June 19, Judge Prescott, who became the spokesman for the men of Ilion, wrote to Lowry, "We have satisfactorily made all the arrangements about the Street Railroad. Tuckerman will be with

Tom Lowry at 32

you in a few days to put the project through with necessary funds to put the line into operation."

Lowry had a reputation for getting things done in a hurry, and the affairs of the streetcar company began to move at a brisk pace. On July 9, the Minneapolis City Council passed an ordinance granting the franchise for the construction, operation, and regulation of two lines. The first, to be completed within four months, was to run from the old St. Paul and Pacific Railroad depot at Washington and Fourth Avenue North, along Washington to Hennepin, thence through Bridge Square, across the Mississippi on the suspension bridge, and on through Southeast Minneapolis to the University of Minnesota. The second line, to be built within one year, was less specific in definition, but called for the Washington Avenue trackage to be extended north to Plymouth, south to Twelfth Avenue South, and then on out to Franklin Avenue, which was the city limit, by the most practical routes available.

In the *Minneapolis Journal* of August 18, 1915, Matt Walsh, a member of the city council, told the story: "Lowry came down to the Council, a stripling of a lad with fire in his eye and humor

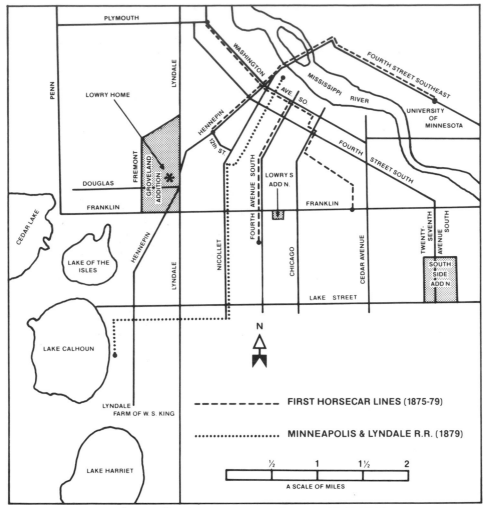

Early Twin Cities Horsecar Routes, 1875-1879

FIRST HORSECAR LINES (1875-79)

MINNEAPOLIS & LYNDALE R.R. (1879)

½   1   1½   2

A SCALE OF MILES

hanging to his lips and a wonderful confidence in the future of Minneapolis, and outside of those things and his great big heart, he had nothing to go on. There were no expert's thoughts necessary in those days of franchise granting. In fact, none but a brave citizen would consent to have a franchise wished off on him. We voted Tom Lowry what he asked for. But I think that if Tom Lowry had been asking for more than he was entitled to, he would have had it just the same, for the kind of man he was would be hard to refuse."

The first two-mile line of streetcar track was to have been laid within four months but was completed in less than half that time.

On August 20, two streetcars arrived from Duluth, having probably come down the Great Lakes waterway. Service on the "University Line" commenced on September 2, 1875. The first day's revenue was $21.50, or 430 five-cent fares.

Lowry's enthusiasm was infectious. On July 16, Judge Prescott had written, "I agree with you about Railroad matters—the sooner the track is laid on Washington Avenue [a reference to the second line] the better. We must not extend the number of owners. We can raise the money to put it through—I will do my share." And on September 11, "I am in favor of at once building a second line. If the people are willing to ride, we of course should be willing to give them the opportunity." Another letter from Prescott to Lowry, dated September 20, reported that King was on his way to Minneapolis with cash and promissory notes from Philo Remington and concluded, "You can say to anyone that Mr. Remington is worth over a million and is an honorable man."

Two more horsecars arrived on September 22 and went right to work. The second line, departing from the specifications of the original franchise, ran down Washington Avenue to Seventh Avenue South, on Seventh Avenue to Fourth Street, and out Fourth Street to Cedar Avenue. In 1876, the council authorized a third line on Hennepin Avenue from Washington to Twelfth Street South; this brought the length of the entire system to about six miles. With the gradual addition of equipment, a 15-minute schedule and a 15-hour day were established for all three lines.

This was not a deluxe transportation system. Since the streets were neither paved nor, in most cases, even graded, the trackage must have been the project of ingenious carpenters with a knack for adapting a road bed to the natural lay of the land. The wooden ties were five inches square and five feet long. Wooden "stringers," also five inches square, were bolted to the ties and then capped with bent iron plate weighing 23 pounds per yard. This was the track, and it cost $6,000 per mile.

The streetcars were 10 feet long (half the length of a large modern automobile) and had two benches which, face to face, would seat 12 to 14 passengers. Weighing 1,000 pounds, each car was drawn by one horse (or mule) at a time, but needed six animals to keep moving for a 15-hour day. At $150 per horse, the capital invested in animals was more than the price of a streetcar, about $750.

In view of the primitive conditions of the streets, to say nothing of the rain, snow, ice, frost, and other elements of Minnesota's climate, it's not surprising that derailments were frequent. Passengers were often asked to assist the driver in putting the half-ton car back on the track, or pushing it up a slippery hill.

There were also problems relating to the motive power, but again the passengers were anxious to help. In the *Minneapolis Tribune* of March 1, 1949, an early driver named Sam Brinker recalled, "Sometimes we'd use mules and sometimes the mules would balk. But none got upset even though the mules were stubborn as long as an hour. Everyone would contribute ideas on how to get

A horsecar used in the Minneapolis Street Railway

them started again. Pulling the tails slowly but steadily was the most popular suggestion."

In winter each car contained a stove and a foot of straw on the floor to keep the passengers' feet from freezing. At night, there were running lights and a smelly kerosene lamp to help the driver count the nickels.

Nor was this pioneer driver a privileged character. Completely unprotected from the elements, he was in his car 15 hours a day with 20 minutes' relief for dinner. He was also expected, either before or after his regular duties, to keep his car scrubbed down inside and out. His pay of $35 per month was not lavish. But if he was mindful of the current slogan, "another day, another dollar," he would consider himself better off than the average, even though the company usually owed him two or three months' back wages.

*   *   *

For the Minneapolis of the 1870s, the three horsecar routes were well located. Washington Avenue, parallel with, but three blocks removed from, the river, was the "Main Street" of the young town. A traveler moving east from Plymouth (Thirteenth Avenue North) and crossing the bridge over Bassett's Creek would find that the first structure of consequence he or she encountered was Lincoln School at Sixth Avenue North. This was one of seven public schools, six parochial schools, and two private schools in Minneapolis. There followed several bleak blocks of shops, blacksmiths, boarding houses, saloons, and a few modest homes, but at Hennepin, Washington Avenue assumed a certain elegance. The Academy of Music, four stories tall with its 1,300-seat theater, was the finest building west of Chicago. On the other side of Hennepin, the Nicollet House not only was the Northwest's leading hotel and social center, but also housed the Farmers and Mechanics Savings Bank and several quality shops. On the other side of Washington, a traveler encountered the First National Bank, the Harrison Block, and the Northwestern National Bank, all housed in thick stone walls, and then the new depot of the Milwaukee Road, where it stands today.

Looking over and beyond the Milwaukee depot, the horsecar passenger could view the real muscle of Minneapolis. Dominating the next several blocks were the mills that were already making Minneapolis known worldwide. Huddled around their source of power, St. Anthony Falls (at Fifth Avenue South), and interwoven by a complex system of dams, waterways, covered canals, sluices, and tailraces, were Charles A. Pillsbury's Anchor Flour Mill, the Washburn A and the Washburn B Flour Mills, and a dozen smaller competitors that were already grinding more than a million barrels of flour a year for the homemakers and bakers of the world. Also tapping the enormous power of the falls were the Morrisons, Eastmans, Boveys, and Walkers, annually sawing the 130 million feet of lumber that was building the Midwest. Other manufacturers included the makers of textiles and farm machinery. The noise from the factories, when combined with the sounds from the cows being driven to pasture, the omnibuses, the carriages, the horsecars, and the people, must have made Washington Avenue a truly raucous thoroughfare.

Turning right at Seventh Avenue and leaving the mills behind, the horsecars proceeded to turn left and run out Fourth Street to the end of the line at Cedar Avenue. To the right lay the more affluent residential areas with their turreted homes of stone and brick, and to the left, the plainer frame homes of the workingmen who doubtless furnished most of the nickel fares.

The University Line left Washington at Hennepin and traversed Bridge Square, which was part of the central business district, although somewhat older and less modern than the rest of it. Conspicuous were the Pence Opera House, the Center Block with the Athenaeum and the City Bank, and the new city hall, which housed the telegraph company and the *Minneapolis Tribune,* successor to Colonel King's original paper. After crossing the bridge, a traveler found Nicollet Island, which offered the contrast of industry on the right and handsome apartment houses and shaded homes on the left. Then, over the river, there rose the imposing Winslow House. Once the summer playground for southerners and their slaves, it was now a Presbyterian college named for its donor, a Mr. Macalester. The business district of old St. Anthony was on Central Avenue and was undistinguished with the exception of the Chute Block at Fourth Street, where the cars turned right and headed for the University of Minnesota. At Fourteenth Avenue Southeast, where the track ended, the campus was only one block distant. In 1878, the university had two buildings and a staff of 15 men and women, including William W. Folwell, who doubled as president and librarian.

Riding the third horsecar line on Hennepin Avenue from Washington down to Twelfth Street, passengers found that a number of handsome residences were still in evidence, including those of lawyer L. M. Stewart and lumberman and library founder T. B. Walker. In every direction were the church spires which were such a conspicuous part of this early landscape. The 1877–78 city directory lists 9 Baptist churches, 4 Catholic churches, 4 Congregational churches, 7 Episcopal churches, 12 Lutheran churches, 13 Methodist churches, and 5 Presbyterian churches, while the Adventists, Quakers, Swedenborgians, and Universalists had 1 church apiece. That makes 58 churches, which should have kept a community of 30,000 people in good order.

*   *   *

By 1877, 18 horsecars were in service, and daily receipts (at five cents per passenger) had gradually increased from the first day's take of $21.50 to $90 and, exceptionally, more than $100 per day. However, the infant company was anything but a gold mine. (See the operating statement, based largely on guesswork, below.)

Fares received (at $90 per day)	$34,675

EXPENSES–1878

Wages—21 drivers	$ 8,820	
Wages—1 blacksmith	600	
Wages—1 maintenance man	600	
Wages—1 horse handler	600	
Wages—1 general manager	1,500	
		12,120
Motive power (108 horses and mules)		
Food at 35¢ per day	13,897	
Shoeing, veterinary, etc., at		
15¢ per day	5,913	
		19,810
Supplies, fuel, maintenance, etc.		2,500
Total expense		$34,430
Funds available for new tracks, new		
equipment, officers' salaries,		
interest, dividends, etc.		$ 245

The streetcar business was less than flourishing, and Colonel King's affairs were considerably worse. With the depression dragging on, money became even tighter, and the market for Minneapolis real estate almost vanished. As the 10 percent and 12 percent interest rates compounded on King's indebtedness, his position became impossible. On October 31, 1877, Lowry, acting as his lawyer, filed a petition in bankruptcy, and on April 8, 1878, King's bankrupt estate was sold to Philo Remington for $50 net, which was probably considerably more than it was worth. Debts were listed at $445,000, and the principal asset was the 1,400-acre Lyndale Farm, which, at a forced sale in 1878, could hardly have brought as much as $200 per acre.

Philo Remington and his Ilion associates had doubtless become disillusioned by their Minneapolis investments. And it was at this time that Lowry formed a syndicate of five Minneapolis men to buy a controlling interest in the streetcar company. A total of $140,000 of the $250,000 stock was purchased and divided equally between Lowry, Clinton Morrison, W. W. McNair (one of the original incorporators), C. H. Prior (superintendent of the Milwaukee Railroad), and H. M. Carpenter (a paper manufacturer). While the details of this transaction are obscure, it probably involved little or no cash, because there wasn't much to be found in Minneapolis in 1878.

Regardless of their cash position, or lack of it, the pioneers of those days had a natural taste for barter. This characteristic is illustrated by the story of the afternoon Beatrice Lowry returned home from shopping, was met on her doorstep by a white-lipped butler, and walked into a drawing room completely stripped of its contents. Gone were the carpets, the tapestries, the draperies, the paintings, the ottomans, the settees, the Tiffany bronzes, and the Tiffany lamps. When Tom Lowry got home a little later, he must

Lowry's drawing room

have been confronted by an agitated wife. But to him it was the most natural thing in the world to swap the contents of a drawing room for a choice piece of real estate which, as it happened, could be acquired in no other way. After all, Mrs. Lowry could always have the drawing room refurnished by Bradstreet's, on credit of course.

The new syndicate probably didn't use furniture to buy the streetcar stock. While it isn't known exactly what they did use, there are some clues to the nature of the transaction. More than half ($75,000) of the stock was bought from Robert L. Innes, as agent for Philo Remington. On June 26, 1878, Lowry deeded to Innes several parcels of Minneapolis real estate, which Innes later deeded to Caroline A. Remington, Philo's wife. Included were several lots in the South Side Addition and one of the Groveland blocks which had been used to buy the Academy of Music and which had been reacquired as a result of Hodges' bankruptcy. So it seems likely the streetcar stock was bought largely with Minneapolis real estate, which, in 1878, would have been about as easy (or hard) to appraise as the streetcar stock which was received in return.

On July 2, 1878, the syndicate elected a new board of directors and the following officers:

President	Thomas Lowry
Vice-president	H. M. Carpenter
Treasurer	T. J. Buxton (treasurer of the City Bank and the city of Minneapolis)
Secretary	C. G. Goodrich, Jr. (Lowry's 22-year-old brother-in-law, who was to become the company's chief operating officer)

For the first time, the company which was to play such an important part in the future of Minneapolis no longer was a creature of Ilion but was in the firm control of Minneapolis men.

Tom Lowry's reasons for throwing himself into the streetcar business are not known. Like King, he may have first been interested in the streetcar's obvious potential for enhancing the value of his outlying real estate. But with his election to the presidency of the company, all his other enterprises became secondary. From that day his all-consuming passion was the streetcar company. Struggling, shabby, unpromising, unprofitable, the business had little apparent allure, and as the years went by, it provided very little return to its owners. But it became a significant force in the growth and shape of the Twin Cities. Perhaps therein could be found Lowry's motives and, in the end, his satisfaction.

Staying All Even

WHEN TOM LOWRY AND HIS PARTNERS BOUGHT CONTROL OF THE streetcar company in the summer of 1878, the depression of the seventies was close to its lowest point. Triggered by the Jay Cooke failure of 1873, the economic slump had dried up foreign and eastern capital and had put the damper on virtually every type of enterprise, including the construction of the railroads, which had been the lifelines of the country's expansion. In Minnesota, whose economy was basically agricultural, the hardship was considerably aggravated by a sudden and mysterious plague of grasshoppers.

During 1873, 1874, and 1875, the first years of the plague, the grasshoppers were concentrated in a few counties, but, in 1876 and 1877, the fields of the entire state were ravaged, and the soil was saturated with eggs which would hatch the following summer. Many of the early settlers gave up and went back east. Those who held out were living on early crops, which matured before the hatch, and on bounty money paid by the state for grasshoppers collected in bushel bags. In the summer of 1877, when the clouds of grasshoppers were at their peak, Governor John S. Pillsbury decreed a statewide day of prayer which was to mark the end of the plague. Within a few days, the grasshoppers started to die, and farmers reported that the insects' bodies were found covered with tiny red mites. In the following summer, Minnesota enjoyed a bumper crop.

As Minnesota agriculture started to revive, Europe headed into a series of crop failures, which meant strong prices for American grain. It also meant a new flood of immigration from the European farmlands to the rich soil of the American Midwest. At the same time, the capital markets were coming back to life, and industry, including the railroads, was beginning to recover. As all of these favorable forces converged on Minneapolis, they resulted in the period of unparalleled growth and development during the years 1880–1893.

The immigrants arriving in Minneapolis in 1880 found a city considerably changed from the town which Tom Lowry first saw in 1867. Population had grown from 10,000 to 45,000. In the central portion of the city, the wooden buildings had been largely replaced by structures of brick and limestone. Streets had been lighted with gas, graded, and bordered by wooden sidewalks. Sewer pipes, nine feet underground, served the center of town and were being extended. There was a wooden water main running down Washington Avenue and across Bridge Square. The value of the buildings standing in 1879 had reached $2,713,000, and, in 1880, the construction under way amounted to $2,000,000, including 26 business blocks worth $257,000, 3 flouring mills for $435,000, and 553 residences costing $952,000.

As the city grew, people kept demanding more and better streetcar services. New track was laid on Fourth Avenue from Washington to the city limits at Franklin; the Washington Avenue Line was extended south along Washington and Riverside to the city limits; a new line served the north side, and another, the northeast section of the city. The earlier lines were lengthened as the residential area expanded. New, larger cars were each now being drawn by two horses, and nine new barns were built throughout the city to house the cars and the animals. The company even operated the "Lowry Elevator" at Fifth Street and Third Avenue North with a capacity of 130,000 bushels of horsepower, more commonly known as oats.

All of these improvements, each demanded by the citizens and ordained by the city council, had to be paid for with new capital, but it wasn't easy to find a capitalist who wanted to invest in a streetcar company which was still earning barely enough to feed its horses.

The story of Tom Lowry's first lesson in high finance is so odd it might be true. It probably happened in 1880, but the following account didn't appear in the *Journal* until 1915:

> It is told of Mr. Lowry that he once thought it would be best for the city if he should sell the system to eastern capitalists who would finance it as it should be financed and make it what it could be made.
>
> So, the story goes, he went to Boston with the intention of selling. The road then was $150,000 in debt. Mr. Lowry concluded that he would be satisfied if he could sell for $400,000. This would leave him and his associates $250,000 for their development work.
>
> When Mr. Lowry had work in sight, he never knew what a holiday was made for. All days and all hours looked alike to him. Midnight was just as good a time to accomplish his object as noon day. He arrived in Boston on a holiday and wandered about the financial district, ready to sell his lines to the highest bidder.
>
> One financial institution after another was found to be closed. Finally Mr. Lowry discovered one place open. A bookkeeper, behind in his work, was spending the holiday catching up. He seemed to be the only soul in the financial district. So Mr. Lowry opened up. Mr. Lowry was not schooled in finance at that time, and he stated bluntly that he had come to Boston to sell a street railway system.
>
> "You have come to the wrong place," confided the bookkeeper laughing. He had been brought up in the financial world.
>
> "It's a good system with a good future. All it needs is capital," declared Mr. Lowry.
>
> "That may all be true, but people down east here don't buy street railroads. In the first place, they are a nuisance to operate. In the second place, if it was any good, you wouldn't want to sell it. What do you want for your lines?"
>
> "I want $400,000," responded Mr. Lowry.

"Well don't try to sell your lines. Keep them yourself. Better bond them for $500,000 here and go home and sell some stock to your home people and you'll have more money and not lose your car lines."

"If you won't give me $400,000 for my railway system, how can I expect to unload $500,000 in bonds and keep the system?" inquired the man from the Northwest.

"Sounds funny, but that's the way things are done in the financial world," replied the bookkeeper.

"Young man," exclaimed Mr. Lowry, "put away your books and come over to my rooms at the hotel. I want to talk to you. I want an education in high finances."

On September 23, 1880, according to its minutes, the Minneapolis Street Railway Company authorized a bond issue of $400,000, of which $150,000 was earmarked to pay existing indebtedness.

About six months later, the minutes of the directors' meeting held on April 13, 1881, contained a lengthy recital of Lowry's many contributions to the company of money, lands, and services. The directors concluded that the company owed Lowry $258,273.50 and would "hereby appropriate said sum to the payment of said indebtedness and [direct] the payment thereof to said Thomas Lowry out of any funds in the treasury of the Corporation."

At about the same time, Lowry's ownership of the company's stock was increased from 1,646 shares to the entire 2,500 shares outstanding. The other stockholders apparently decided they would rather take their shares in cash and let Lowry have the stock. Thus Lowry became the sole owner of the Minneapolis Street Railway Company. If Lowry was right when he valued the company at $400,000, his stock, after the deduction of the $400,000 bond issue, should have been worth exactly nothing. But for better or worse, his education in "high finance" had been promptly put in practice.

*　　*　　*

St. Paul's streetcar system had a history even more turbulent and unpromising than that of its Minneapolis counterpart. The St. Paul company was organized by St. Paul businessmen in 1872, and its properties were foreclosed by a group of 13 New York bondholders in 1877. The company's assets included 3¾ miles of track, 15 cars, 34 horses, 6 mules, 24 horse collars, 14 bridles, 16 horse blankets, 4 buffalo robes, 3 pitchforks, 9 coal stoves for the cars, 3 monkey wrenches, and 2 mouth rasps for the horses' teeth.

The new owners were destined for a painful experience in the streetcar business. Their resident manager was James R. Walsh, and his first move was to increase the fare from five cents to six cents. Soon thereafter, a woman who had only a nickel was thrown off a car by an overzealous driver, and she promptly filed suit for $1,500. A few months later the suit was settled for $200, and the directors reluctantly concurred in Walsh's plea to return the fare to five cents.

The New Yorkers approved several minor extensions of the system and the construction of a new building on St. Peter Street to house both staff and animals. The operation was yielding a return of 7 to 8 percent on the $77,000 investment, but when one of the directors traveled to St. Paul to inspect the property in the fall of 1879, he brought back a discouraging report. The original rails had been too light amd were worn out, while the ties were decayed "almost to punk."

After considerable soul-searching, the New Yorkers regathered their courage and decided to put in an additional $50,000 to rebuild and expand the system. The actual cost of the improvements proved to be $85,000, which was financed by selling $73,000 in new stock and borrowing $12,000 from one of the stockholders. Outstanding stock now amounted to $150,000, and the 1880 net income of $9,000 was only about half of the 12 to 14 percent return which had been forecast. To forestall a competitor, the company was forced to build a new line on Rice Street in early 1881 and found it impossible to declare the semiannual dividend payable in August.

Short of cash and harassed by unforeseen outlays, the New Yorkers felt their enthusiasm for this remote investment rapidly declining.

On February 11, 1882, in an office at 90 Broadway in New York City, the St. Paul City Railway Company was turned over to a new group of owners: Francis B. Clarke, president of the Northwestern Manufacturing and Car Company, Herman Greve, a real estate dealer, Ansel Oppenheim, an investment broker, William R. Merriam, vice-president of the Merchants National Bank and future governor of Minnesota, and Thomas Lowry. With the exception of Lowry, all of the new owners were St. Paul businessmen, and each bought one-fifth of the 1,500 shares of stock outstanding. Clarke was elected president; Greve, vice-president; and Merriam, secretary-treasurer.

The first action of the new board of directors was to authorize Lowry, who had become versed in the ways of "high finance," to negotiate a first mortgage loan of $200,000. As soon as they obtained the loan, the directors, in a meeting held June 24, 1882, voted to pay $177,000 to the five new stockholders as compensation for the time and energy they had devoted to reorganizing and acquiring the new company. In other words, the new loan reimbursed the new stockholders for the cost of their stock.

The loan also provided for an additional $300,000 to be borrowed by the company at the rate of $10,000 for each mile of new track to be laid in the future. St. Paul was now experiencing the same surge of immigration and growth that Minneapolis was, and, with the funds provided by the mortgage loan, the St. Paul horsecar system was rapidly expanded. But once again the earnings fell short of expectation. In addition to paying operating expenses, the company was now faced with paying out 6 percent interest on its new indebtedness. At the annual meeting of January 15, 1883, the minutes noted: "The road having been operated at a loss, the matter of dividends was not brought up."

The St. Paul stockholders soon lost interest in their new investment, which seemed to be worth what they had paid for it—i.e., nothing. In July 1883, Clark, Greve, and Oppenheim resigned from the board and were replaced by Lowry's brother-in-law, C. G. Goodrich, and his old friend, Clinton Morrison. The new board promptly elected Tom Lowry president of the St. Paul City Railway Company, and the St. Paul men presumably sold their stock to the Minneapolis associates at the same time at a price which was not recorded and was probably not substantial.

Tom Lowry's reasons for entering St. Paul are a matter of conjecture. The prospects of the Minneapolis streetcar system may have been bleak, but the outlook for its St. Paul counterpart was even bleaker. And since the two systems were separated by five miles of open country, they had very little in common except for their dismal financial records. Perhaps Lowry foresaw the day when the two cities would grow together and the two systems could be joined; or perhaps he couldn't resist the challenge to improve a situation which was even worse than his own. He may also have been intrigued by the fact that St. Paul, with a population about equal to that of Minneapolis, was providing transportation for less than half as many horsecar riders. And St. Paul was experiencing, though to a lesser degree, the same sort of stunning growth which was occurring on the other side of the river. So the prospects may have been brighter than the operating deficits would have indicated.

When the New Yorkers sold out in 1882, Lowry's part in the transaction was apparently unknown to the public. But when, in 1883, he made his appearance as president and dominant stockholder in the St. Paul City Railway Company, a furor developed in the St. Paul business community. Rivalry and hostility between the two cities had reached a new high, and the initial reaction of St. Paulites was shock. Years later, in an article that recalled Tom Lowry's personality, the *St. Paul Dispatch* gave the following account:

> The idea of a Minneapolis man having us at his mercy when
> it came to street cars was so repugnant to many of our people
> that J. W. McClung, a leading real estate dealer, called an in-

dignation meeting at the Chamber of Commerce. That was precisely what the assemblage was to be—"mad clear through"—notwithstanding the circumstance that Tom Lowry was expected to attend in person and defend himself, were self-defense possible, which was doubted seriously. Mr. McClung was primed for an oration of the most scorching and withering type, with the street railway magnate as the cowering, totally silenced victim. That a Philistine, an arch-enemy of St. Paul as every Minneapolitan must be perforce, should gobble our street railroad franchises and privileges, was an outrage.

Mr. Lowry duly appeared upon the scene and laid aside the inevitable plug hat which so accentuated his six feet two. He faced that angry audience and smiled. Half the anger vanished forthwith. Tom kept on facing the audience and smiling, and then he talked a little while. He presented a full exposition of his plans and desires regarding the St. Paul street car system.

And then what happened? Nothing, except that J. W. McClung got on his legs and started eulogizing that terrible Tom Lowry! Applause began to ripple forth as he went on. The acclaim gathered force and swelled until it made the old building tremble and the captive, turned captor, received a tumultuous ovation whose like is seldom witnessed except perhaps in a political meeting during a heated campaign.

Lowry had won another victory. Those who came to curse remained to bless and went away to respect and love. He had tapped the hearts of the St. Paulites as deftly as he had tapped the strongboxes of Wall Street.

Lowry's next move in St. Paul was to increase the company's bonded debt to $1,000,000, enabling him to pay off the $350,000 bonds then outstanding, to pay other debts of $300,000 incurred in recent extensions, and to spend $350,000 in additional improvements of the system.

The net result of the St. Paul acquisition was that Lowry had two loads to carry instead of one, and each was steadily growing in weight. But burdens didn't bother him in that booming era of the eighties. He had reached his fortieth birthday in 1883, and was possessed of good health and high spirits. He never appeared to lose his sense of humor or his delight in the ridiculous; he was apparently having a wonderful time.

A close friend of the family used to tell of the day the news raced through town that Tom Lowry was bankrupt. It might have been the day in early 1881 that an eastern investor foreclosed his delinquent mortgage on the Lowry home, or it might have been one of the many other occasions when it seemed that the sheriff had finally caught up with Tom. In any event, the old friend made his way to Groveland Terrace and, approaching the front door, was trying to choose his words of condolence, dreading his entrance into the household of a ruined man. As the door opened, he was greeted with roars of laughter, squeals of delight, and the sight of Tom Lowry and his two young daughters racing through the halls and galleries in a game of tag.

Laughter was the rule in the house on Lowry Hill, and Tom never tired of teasing his beautiful and stylish wife. If there were 20 guests seated at a formal dinner, Lowry might have Henry, the German butler, slip him a worn-out napkin. Thrusting his thumb

A hallway in the Lowry home

through a hole, he would brandish the napkin over his head and shout down the length of the great table, "Trice, dear, can't we really afford something better than this?"

On another occasion, he came home announcing that he had enjoyed an unexpected windfall and presented his wife with three $100 bills. He urged her to go on a shopping spree the next morning. When the clerk at Bradstreet's informed her that the money was counterfeit, Trice was furious and demanded $300 in genuine currency, which Tom had to borrow from a friend.

Lowry always boasted that his aim in life was to stay all even, by which he meant owing money to as many men as he didn't owe money. But no one ever doubted his honesty or his intention to pay his debts in due time, and no one ever failed to get paid—although sometimes people had to have patience. In this period of the city's development, Lowry's supreme optimism was an important asset. Without it, some of Minneapolis' proudest triumphs could not have been achieved, and one of these was the West Hotel.

A City's Growth

THE WEST HOTEL WAS BUILT BY CHARLES W. WEST OF CINCINNATI, whose interest in Minneapolis had been cultivated by John T. West, his favorite nephew, and Thomas Lowry. John T. West was at the time lessee and manager of the Nicollet House. And it was probably Tom Lowry, the tireless promoter of his community, who persuaded Charles W. West to build the West Hotel as a princely gift to his nephew and as a unique contribution to the development of Minneapolis. For a year or two, it was perhaps the finest hotel west of Chicago.

The site for the hotel, 174 feet on Hennepin Avenue and 196 feet on Fifth Street North, was owned by Schuyler H. Mattison, whose real estate office was in Room 2 of the Academy of Music. Thomas Lowry, of Room 1 of the Academy of Music, negotiated Mattison's sale of the site to Charles W. West for $45,000 by a warranty deed dated September 24, 1881, on which Lowry's name appears as a witness. On February 8, 1882, Charles West deeded the property to his nephew, and, on March 22, 1883, Lowry laid the cornerstone with appropriate ceremonies. General supervision of the construction was entrusted by the Wests to Lowry.

Designed by Minneapolis architect L. S. Buffington, the hotel consisted of eight floors which contained spacious dining rooms and other public areas, 407 bedrooms with hot and cold running water, and 150 bathrooms. With massive walls of marble, brick, and terra cotta, and with floors and ceilings of fireclay tile, the structure was

The West Hotel, the finest hotel west of Chicago in the 1880s. Tom Lowry was one of its principal promoters.

completely fireproof. The lighting was furnished by Swan incandescent bulbs and the Owsle storage battery system. Interior surfaces were liberally decorated with marble and mahogany woodwork, and a large interior court added to the spaciousness of the rooms. The cost was $1,500,000, or some $500,000 more than original estimates. Charles W. West was determined to give his nephew and Minneapolis an outstanding facility.

The hotel was opened to the public during the summer of 1884, and after several months of shakedown, the formal ceremonies were scheduled. Some say that Minneapolis came of age at eight o'clock on the evening of November 19, 1884, when 356 public officials, businessmen, and other prominent Twin Citians assembled for the dedication. The ceremony was a splendid tribute to the founders of the West Hotel, and it also served as a testimony to the hardiness and stamina of the participants.

Gathering in the hotel's rotunda for an hour of "agreeable intercourse," the throng moved in to dinner at nine o'clock. It took half an hour to seat the guests, who had paid $10 a plate, at the carefully place-carded tables. An 11-course dinner, washed down with four wines, was served by 150 waiters in full dress. The eating went on for three hours, and the speeches, which began at 12:30, lasted until 2:40 in the morning.

The hotel's proprietor, John West, sat at one end of the head table, and Thomas Lowry, its principal promoter, sat at the other, while W. D. Washburn served as toastmaster. There were four additional tables, which seated 42 men on each side, including virtually all of the leading men of Minneapolis and St. Paul. Governor Hubbard was flanked by former Governor John S. Pillsbury and University President Cyrus Northrop, along with St. Paul Mayor C. D. O'Brien and Minneapolis Mayor George A. Pillsbury. Miller Charles A. Pillsbury sat across the table from realtor Sam Gale. There were many identified with the burgeoning railroad industry, including James J. Hill, who was introduced by Mayor O'Brien as St. Paul's first and honored citizen. The banks were represented by the Sidles of the First National, Hugh Harrison and F. A. Chamberlain of the Security, and S. A. Harris and W. E. Burwell (whose daughter would marry Tom Lowry's son) from the Northwestern. Lumbermen T. B. Walker, W. W. Eastman, C. A. Bovey, and John deLaittre were there. The legal profession was represented by Judge Atwater, Judge Koon, Judge Young, and W. H. Eustis. Tom Lowry's old friends, William S. King and Dr. H. H. Kimball, sat together, as did partners T. B. Janney and F. B. Semple. C. M. Loring, George Brackett, A. C. Rand, W. H. Northrup, C. W. Case, J. S. Bradstreet, Anthony Kelly, F. C. Pillsbury, E. J. Phelps—virtually every prominent citizen could be found in the West Hotel that notable evening. A few had the foresight to reserve a room for the night.

As the guests sat down and the waiters started serving the oysters and pouring the haute sauterne, the conversation turned from small talk to more substantive topics. Almost every man present was deeply involved in the dramatic growth which had swept up two small towns and was, within a few brief years, remaking them into a metropolitan area. No one really knows what was discussed that night at the West Hotel, but the prominent citizens attending the dinner must have talked long and vigorously about the present and future of Minneapolis and St. Paul. Their conversation may have proceeded along these lines:

At the center of the head table, Cyrus Northrop, newly appointed President of the university, spoke with John S. Pillsbury, who, for the past 30 years, had been the university's strongest friend. Northrop expressed pleasure and surprise at the number of prominent St. Paul men who had crossed the river to attend this Minneapolis celebration. (While the university was on Minneapolis ground, it was located on the St. Paul side of the river.) A newcomer from his professorship at Yale University, Northrop revealed his disappointment at the lack of cooperation between the two cities.

Governor Pillsbury, a long-time student of this subject, tried to explain some of the reasons for the cities' mutual antagonism.

"You have to remember," Pillsbury said, "that St. Paul was here first. When I settled in St. Anthony in 1855, St. Paul was the unquestioned center of this whole region and Minneapolis didn't even exist. At the head of navigation on the Mississippi, St. Paul naturally attracted the fur traders and later the shippers and the warehousemen who were supplying the needs of the whole territory. St. Paul was the only logical choice for the capital of the state in 1858—there wasn't any other town that approached it in size or importance. So the people of St. Paul got used to being top dog. And they naturally resent the fact that Minneapolis is now larger and growing faster than they are. Next year's census will probably put St. Paul at about 110,000 and Minneapolis at around 130,000.

"To make matters worse, both cities have sometimes been less than considerate of each other. For example, Minneapolis boasts of the purity of its water supply, pointing out that its water is drawn

from the Mississippi at the northern edge of the city and that its
sewage is returned to the river at a point well below the intake. If
you were living downstream in St. Paul, you might find this proce-
dure rather irritating, to say the least."

Pillsbury went on to explain that a further source of dissension
could be found in the fact that St. Paulites and Minneapolitans
were "different breeds of cat." Many of St. Paul's early settlers and
founders had come up the river from the South, and its first society
had been influenced by the officers of Fort Snelling, many of whom
were southerners. In sharp contrast were the New Englanders,
with their puritan ethic, who had been drawn to St. Anthony Falls
by their appetite for water power and lumber.

"To complete the contrast, St. Paul has a large population of
Irish and German Catholics imported to build the railroads, while
the Minneapolis workman is more apt to be a Scandinavian Lutheran. In looking at a Twin Cities business directory recently, I
noticed that Minneapolis has about 300 saloons compared with 600
saloons in St. Paul.

"Those cosmopolitan people across the river think of us as a
bunch of Swedes and damn Yankees—and upstarts as well," said
Pillsbury, who himself had come from New Hampshire.

Dr. Northrop, who had been listening intently, smiled. "I don't
think we should call them the Twin Cities—it's a misnomer," he
said. "Twins are born at the same time and these cities were not.
Perhaps the 'Sibling Cities' would be a better term."

At another table, St. Paul's foremost citizen spoke about his favorite subject—the romance of the railroads. James J. Hill was a
powerful man. Set on a short, squat frame, his large head with its
one good eye was almost hypnotic. He developed the theme that
railroads, like perpetual motion, were a closed-circuit source of energy and growth. The railroads were built by immigrant laborers
who settled on the adjacent land to grow wheat. The railroads
hauled the wheat east to pick up more loads of manufactured goods
and more immigrants to build more trackage, grow more wheat,

buy more goods, and make more jobs. In Mr. Hill's view of the scene, what was good for the railroads was good for Minnesota.

Colonel King was sitting across the table from Hill, and as the waiters were removing the oyster shells and serving the soup (creme de volaille), the colonel found the opportunity to turn the conversation to his favorite railroad. While he had lost control of the Minneapolis Street Railway Company, King had found another means of connecting his Lyndale Farm with the population of Minneapolis. Working with Philo Remington's agents, who had a common interest in the Lyndale Farm, King had persuaded a Colonel McCrory of Columbus, Ohio, to incorporate the Lyndale Railway Company, and he had talked his old friend, Tom Lowry, into leasing to this new company the street railway right-of-way from Bridge Square out First Avenue South and Nicollet Avenue to Lake Calhoun, where the colonel had built a small hotel known as the Pavillion. The steam-powered railroad, known as the Motor Line, started running six trains a day to Lake Calhoun in the sum-

The Lyndale and Minnetonka Railroad, also known as the Motor Line

mer of 1879 and soon extended its tracks to Lake Harriet and Lake Minnetonka. It wasn't much of a railroad, but any sort of transportation was a potent factor in that period, and the Motor Line had proven to be a real force in the development of the lakes and the enhancement of the value of Colonel King's property. The colonel had just filed a lawsuit against Remington to recover his rights to Lyndale Farm, which had seemed so hopelessly burdened with debt. The Motor Line was integrated with the streetcar company only three years later.

As the soup was being cleared and replaced by pompano fillets, Charles Pillsbury replied to Sam Gale's studious questions about the new technology of the flour mills, which were the chief pride of Minneapolis. The explosion of the Washburn A Mill on May 2, 1878, which destroyed most of the flour mills on the west side of the river, had already proven to be a blessing in disguise. Larger and more modern facilities had quickly replaced the old mills. Flour ground in the old way by millstones from the hard northern spring wheat had compared poorly with flour ground from the softer wheats of Kansas and Missouri. But the new mills were equipped with steel rollers and middlings purifiers which gradually reduced the hard wheat to the finest flour in the world. With larger and more efficient mills and with a growing wheat harvest along the railroad tracks of Minnesota and the Dakota Territory, Minneapolis was now producing 5 million barrels of superior flour per year compared with 1 million barrels of marginal-quality flour in the year before the explosion. Minneapolis was becoming the flour capital of the world.

The capon and terrapin had come and gone, the filet de boeuf was being served, and T. B. Walker was being queried about the other great industry which was building Minneapolis. Always modest, Walker was slow to admit that his mills would saw 300 million feet of lumber during that year, to say nothing of the lathes and shingles, the slabs for the stoves, and the sawdust which fired the boilers to make the steam to run the saws.

Throughout all these conversations ran the exciting theme of growth—the surge of migrants who had changed Minneapolis, in 10 short years, from a town of 25,000 to a city of 125,000. Real estate values had revived, new homes were mushrooming, and, as new neighborhoods formed, their first demands were for horsecar lines. As the canvasbacks were passed and the champagne was poured, Tom Lowry painted his vision of a great Twin Cities metropolis laced with the gleaming tracks of the world's finest transportation system.

The evening's speeches were uniformly polished, witty, and to the point. Three general themes ran through most of the oratory.

The first theme was gratitude to Charles West, who had given Minneapolis this magnificent civic asset. The head table was dominated by a huge, solid silver vase, three feet high, made by Tiffany and Company and purchased for $5,000 by the city fathers as a token of their appreciation. On one side of the vase was a large image of the bearded Mr. West and on the other side, an engraving of the hotel; on the base was a horsecar, perhaps a tribute to Tom Lowry's part in the hotel's construction. Due to the untimely death of Charles West two months before the dedication, the vase was presented to John West with appropriate exhortations that he make the hotel everything his uncle had desired it to be.

The second theme was gratitude to Thomas Lowry, who had been the catalyst in the creation of the hotel. While the details of the West-Lowry relationship are not clear, there was no question that Lowry had been the guiding force. John West included in his speech the following tribute. (The speeches were published in the banquet program, *Formal Opening of the West Hotel.*)

> Nor can I, on this occasion, fail to publicly thank one who, next to the founder of this hotel, has done so much for Minneapolis and myself—a gentleman whom everyone present hails as a friend, and who has, as my advisor and advocate, proven a friend indeed. From the earliest thought of building a hotel here, down to the present moment, he has been never tiring,

but always ready and anxious to do more; many trips has he made away from the city in the interest of this hotel, giving his time and neglecting his own business, doing anything and everything to encourage and assist me and advance the interests of the city he loves so well, and all this without any pecuniary interest, and without thought of fee or reward. How to sufficiently thank him I know not—I cannot find words to express my gratitude to the man who has uniformly declared that he would "stand by John until the hotel is finished and every obligation satisfied." You all know to whom I refer, but you do not know how much he has done, or the struggle of the past few months. One thing we all know: The City of Minneapolis, the West Hotel and ourselves never had a better friend than the tried and true, genial Thomas Lowry.

The "struggle of the past few months" must have included solving a shortage of funds resulting from the difference between the final cost of $1,500,000 and the original estimate of $1,000,000. A clue can be found in a mortgage for $400,000 given to Farmers' Loan and Trust Company of New York City by John West on July 1, 1884, and also a lien on the hotel filed by architect L. S. Buffington, who had received only $5,000 of his $45,000 bill for services rendered. This financial "struggle" was the kind with which Tom Lowry was quite familiar.

The third theme of the speeches was a call for more cooperation between the two cities, coupled with condemnation of their traditional attitude of suspicion and jealousy. These sentiments were expressed with great conviction by men from both sides of the river. University President Cyrus Northrop put it this way:

I have not found in Minnesota, since I have been here, any evidence of foolishness except one; and if you will allow me, a comparative newcomer, placed here in your midst by force of circumstances, to tell you frankly what that is, it is the seeming jealousy which has existed between Minneapolis and St. Paul. — I trust that this occasion of the formal opening of the West Hotel will ever be remembered by the citizens of St. Paul and Minneapolis as the occasion upon which the noble groom and the beautiful bride were so happily united never to be sundered. — Why, Sir, here are two cities, each of them magnificent, each of them beautiful, each of them prosperous beyond all precedent, and what in the name of common sense are they wrangling about? Each of them has enough. They are destined in the near future to become one.

James J. Hill put it more bluntly:

The time has come when the cities of Minneapolis and St. Paul can work together for their mutual advantage and advancement. If these cities are true to themselves, if they are true to their own interests, there is no rival they need fear. The future will be greater than the past. Although I live in St. Paul, I think I can fairly judge of the interests and motives of both places; and I say to you tonight that I have never yet been able to find out what it is about, except that one fellow "said it," or one fellow "did it" and the other "must meet him." I think the time has come when both cities have outgrown their swaddling clothes, and they must lay them aside, and in the future they must stand side by side for themselves. — No one here tonight who will take the question home to himself will deny that the future of these cities will be greater if we work together for our mutual advantage.

Mayor O'Brien predicted the union of the two cities and went so far as to say:

From that union there will spring a stately structure, raising its white dome and rearing it beyond the clouds. Upon that dome shall rest the sacred figure of liberty with hand forever pointing towards heaven that sent and protects her for the benefit of the Republic. Beneath that dome shall assemble the wisdom and the sages of the nation, and at its base, in wide and far extending vistas, shall reach out the stately city which shall be first in patriotism, first in learning, first in arts and sciences, first in commerce and manufactures—the future Capital of the United States of America.

While Thomas Lowry's remarks were directed largely to the benefactions of Charles West, he also added his word to the theme of union: "As against St. Paul and Minneapolis united, with one common interest, Nature has provided no rival. In fact we have everything to make this, these two cities, one great and grand metropolis." While his oratory on the subject was not as prolonged as those of some of the other speakers, Lowry was perhaps the only man in the room to have actually done something about bringing the cities together. And in the years ahead, he was to do a great deal more.

Lowry at age 40

This photograph of the Northwestern National Bank was taken in 1890. In 1883, Lowry was elected one of its directors.

Side Interests

THERE WERE MANY "WEST HOTELS" IN TOM LOWRY'S LIFE. WHILE
they all became secondary to his preoccupation with the streetcar
business, he was constantly engaged in side interests which absorbed considerable time and energy. It was impossible for him to
refuse a friend who asked for help with any new venture which
could contribute to the growth and welfare of Minneapolis. Since
his friends were many and their imaginations prolific, Lowry was
always involved in a stunning multiplicity of human affairs. A few
examples will illustrate the breadth and diversity of his interests.

Lowry was identified with banking as early as 1872, when, as a
young lawyer, he inscribed the minutes of the first stockholders
meeting of Northwestern National Bank, of which Dr. Goodrich
was an original incorporator and director. Lowry was elected a director of the bank in 1883. The articles of incorporation of another
bank, the Farmers and Mechanics, were signed in Lowry's office in
the Academy of Music in 1874. An original trustee of that bank, he
also served as an inactive vice-president from 1886 until his death.

Soon after resolving the many problems of the West Hotel,
Lowry became involved in another public enterprise. In 1885,
through the cooperative effort of the Minneapolis Athenaeum (a
private library), the Minnesota Academy of Science, and the Minneapolis City Council, a public library was formed. The city agreed
to furnish $100,000 through the sale of bonds on the condition that
$50,000 be contributed by the public. Lowry was one of eight men

who each contributed $5,000 toward the public fund, which came to total $61,000. Along with president and prime mover T. B. Walker, Lowry was a member of the first library board. He was also named chairman of the building committee which undertook the planning and construction of the first public library at Tenth Street and Hennepin Avenue. The library was opened on December 16, 1889, and in the display area of the Academy of Science on the third floor, the most conspicuous exhibit consisted of the two articles which are the subject of the following letter written on stationery from Cook's Nile Steamboat Service:

> On the Nile
> Luxor, Egypt
> December 23, 1886

Professor W. W. Folwell
Minneapolis, Minnesota

My dear Professor:

My little boy has been very anxious since our arrival in Egypt to see a live mummy. I consoled him by saying that his father was as near an approach to it as he was likely to find. Thinking that perhaps many of our Minnesota children would be equally curious on the mummy question, I today bought two very fine ones, all complete and intact as taken from the tomb. I have ordered them sent to you to be presented to the Academy of Science of Minneapolis. There may be some difficulty in getting them out of Egypt, as the authorities are very strict, I am told, about taking such things out of the country. But I think I have arranged it through our Consul so that there will be no delay. Hoping they will arrive safely and be acceptable I am

> Your friend,
> Thomas Lowry

Another early dream of Minneapolis men was a direct connection with the East which would be independent of the great railroad hub of Chicago. Toward this end, the Soo Line was incorporated in 1883 by W. D. Washburn along with such leaders as H. T. Welles, C. M. Loring, Clinton Morrison, Charles Pillsbury, and Lowry. The first section, to Turtle Lake, Wisconsin, was completed in 1885. The road reached Rhinelander in 1886 and was pushed through to Sault Ste. Marie in 1887, 496 miles in all. Here it joined a new track of the Canadian Pacific, which ran through Canada to Montreal and on to Portland and Boston. After the Soo Line had been acquired by the Canadian Pacific, Lowry in 1889 was named president and served in that capacity until his death.

The Minneapolis Stockyards and Packing Company, formed in 1887, was destined to bring financial trauma to the lives of many Minneapolitans, but during its early years, it was a roaring success. Its objective was to draw livestock business away from Chicago and to process cattle closer to their points of origin. Charles Pillsbury and Thomas Lowry each subscribed $50,000 to the original capital of $1 million. One thousand acres of land were acquired in New Brighton and two large packinghouses were erected. The new Belt Line Railroad was built to connect the stockyards with the Minnesota Transfer Railroad and the Great Northern and Northern Pacific. This enterprise got off to a flying start and, under the direction of George Brackett, was regarded as one of the important factors in the city's economic development.

Lowry's interest in the development of medical education probably had its roots in his old friendship with Dr. Kimball and his relationship to Dr. Goodrich. This interest was ultimately utilized by one Dr. Fred Dunsmoor, a bright young man who had formed a passion for surgery while dissecting animals on the family farm in Richfield. At 16, he began "reading medicine" in the Harrison Block offices of Drs. Goodrich and Kimball. He then spent three years taking the full course of New York's Bellevue Hospital College. Returning to Minneapolis with his M.D. in 1876, Dunsmoor began practice in partnership with Dr. Kimball, and he served as professor of surgery at the St. Paul Medical School. Convinced that local medical education had to have clinical facilities, he conceived the idea of a combined medical college and free hospital, to be known as the Minnesota College Hospital. Enlisting the support of several leading doctors, Dunsmoor prevailed on Tom Lowry to be the president. Private money was raised to buy the old Winslow House, which was being vacated by Macalester College, and here the new institution with 100 beds was founded in 1881. The first facility of its kind in the Midwest, the college was a great success and was later one of the founding members of the University of Minnesota Medical School.

Shortly after the founding of the Minnesota College Hospital, Beatrice Lowry became involved in starting a different type of medical facility. On November 3, 1882, Harriet Walker, the wife of library founder and lumberman T. B. Walker, called together a group of friends to discuss the need for a new hospital to be managed by women, for the care of indigent women and children, and for the training of nurses. On November 6, Northwestern Hospital for Women and Children was incorporated with a board of trustees composed entirely of women. Harriet Walker was elected president and Beatrice Lowry vice-president.

A small house at 2504 Fourth Avenue South was purchased for $3,000, and the ladies undertook to furnish it through contribution of the necessary materials. The first annual report lists contributions by 161 individuals and businesses such as 10 pounds of feathers, a spring bed, and other furniture from Phelps and Bradstreet; a coal stove, bedspreads, table linen, dishes, and a dozen silver spoons from Mrs. H. H. Kimball; seven pairs of blankets from the North Star Woolen Mills; two barrels of flour from Dorilus Morrison; and a chamber set, a bed, a carpet, and a pair of feather pillows from Mrs. John S. Pillsbury. Harriet Walker and Beatrice Lowry were among the 154 people who made cash contributions ranging from 50 cents to $500, providing $3,975 toward purchasing and furnishing the 18-bed hospital. Soon thereafter lawyer "Elder" Stewart donated property at Chicago Avenue and Twenty-

Seventh Street valued at $20,000, and the ladies built, furnished, and operated a new 50-bed hospital at a cost of $40,000.

The Northwestern Knitting Company provided still further variety in Lowry's interests. In 1887, inventor George D. Munsing, whose Munsingwear underwear was to become world famous, induced Lowry, Charles Pillsbury, and Clinton Morrison to provide badly needed capital for his newly formed textile factory. According to Shutter's history of Minneapolis, "the arguments used, as the early records indicate, were those of advancing the industrial development of Minneapolis. Civic pride and the ambition to stimulate the industrial growth of Minneapolis induced these men of affairs to back the struggling little company."

Probably the most colorful and the most hazardous of Lowry's many sidelines were the Guaranty Loan building and the Northwestern Guaranty Loan Company, both of which were the brainchildren of Louis Francois Menage. Even as Minneapolis bragged in 1884 of the West as the finest hotel in the land, so the Guaranty Loan building, completed in 1890, was hailed as the country's grandest office building. Its 12 stories, located at Third Street and Second Avenue South, housed the Northwestern and Security Banks, the Soo Line, and the Milwaukee Road. The first three stories were of green granite, the upper nine of red sandstone; all four sides were finished alike. The building boasted six passenger elevators, 3,000 incandescent bulbs, and 15 arc lights. The Northwestern Guaranty Loan Company was engaged in every sort of real estate transaction, including the sale of debentures, secured by "guaranteed" mortgages, which became well regarded in eastern financial circles. Menage was backed by the same group of tireless promoters of Minneapolis growth. Among the directors of his companies were Lowry, Charles and George Pillsbury, Senator Washburn, C. H. Pettit, and W. H. Eustis. Lowry, an inactive vicepresident, little suspected the financial fate that would ultimately befall Menage.

On top of his basic commitment to the streetcar business and his

The Guaranty Loan Building (1890) was hailed as the country's grandest office building. Financially, it proved one of the most hazardous of Lowry's many side interests.

participation in these outside interests, Lowry never lost his love of real estate. Three of his principal ventures illustrate the effort and imagination which he put into this lifelong pursuit.

When the Academy of Music was destroyed by fire on Christmas Day of 1884, it was still the property of Tom Lowry and the Herrick Brothers. Before its ashes were cold, the owners had started planning the construction of a new building to occupy the same prime site on the corner of Hennepin and Washington Avenues. Designed by architect E. Townsend Mix, the new eight-story building was constructed of granite, terra cotta, and brownstone, and it was said to be absolutely fireproof. Completed in 1886 at a cost of $250,000, Temple Court was the premiere office building in town until Menage opened the Guaranty Loan building four years later.

Lowry made another successful real estate acquisition in downtown St. Paul. The original car barn and office of the St. Paul City Railway Company was located on the east side of St. Peter Street between Fourth and Fifth Streets, and after fire destroyed it, Lowry began purchasing the greater part of this city block. In 1889, he bought five lots for $180,000 from the estate of W. F. Davidson, and, on September 18, 1890, he bought the two lots lying along St. Peter Street from the streetcar company for $100,000, which would seem to have been a full price for the property. While the site was only modestly improved during Tom Lowry's life, his son, Horace, in later years, developed the block into a successful complex which included the Lowry Medical Arts Buildings, the Lowry Hotel, and the Field-Schlick department store.

Lowry's other major real estate effort was to prove less successful. Convinced that the trend of residential development would prove to be northeastward, he envisioned a "new town" rather like the more recent concept of Jonathan, Minnesota (a totally self-contained, planned community). During the 1880s, Lowry gradually accumulated some 800 acres of land in the area between Main Street, Central Avenue, and Thirty-Third and Forty-Fifth Avenues Northeast at a cost of about $70,000. In 1892, he organized the Minneapolis Improvement Company Northeast, which took title to this property and acquired an additional 200 acres from other owners. One hundred and thirty-two acres were sold to the Minneapolis Park Board for inclusion in a new park named Columbia Park (because it had been formed in the Columbian Year). When the balance of the property was platted for development, it was named Columbia Heights.

Columbia Heights was laid out as a self-contained community with 200 acres for industrial sites connected to Soo Line trackage and 700 acres for homesites, in addition to Columbia Park on its southeast corner. The tract lay north of the growing city, which was only a few minutes distant by electric streetcar. Everyone thought that the development was sure to flourish and was not surprised that Lowry had bought an adjoining section of 640 acres for $200,000 to hold for future development. It was one more reason for the *Tribune* to include Tom Lowry as one of 15 Minneapolis men who were undoubtedly millionaires. And there is little doubt that Lowry was a millionaire on the basis of an 1892 valuation of his assets. But his million dollars was never invested in anything as mundane as cash.

In addition to his commercial ventures, Lowry had a lifelong interest in politics. Ever since the days of Colonel King's *Atlas,* he had been an ardent booster of the Republican Party, the party of his idol, Abraham Lincoln. When his Republican friends undertook to secure the 1892 Republican National Convention for Minneapolis, Lowry gave full support to the effort. John T. West and Lowry each contributed $5,000 toward the expenses of the committee, and Lowry was among the men who went to Washington to plead the Minneapolis case before the Republican National Committee. Their success in obtaining the convention was hailed as the first national recognition of Minneapolis as a city of the first class.

A more active political role for Lowry might have resulted from the unexpected death of the secretary of the treasury of the United

States during the same hectic year of 1891. The secretary was William Windom, a former Republican senator from Minnesota, and some of Lowry's friends urged that he be appointed as Windom's successor. The *New York Times* of March 28, 1891, ran the following:

> There is an interesting story in connection with Mr. Lowry's failure to secure the appointment. It is said that the President [Harrison] was told of certain of Mr. Lowry's actions when elated over political success and ceased his consideration at that moment. When W. D. Washburn was a candidate for the Senate, Mr. Lowry managed his campaign. When Washburn was elected [in 1889], Mr. Lowry felt so good that he became very demonstrative. He is a very tall, thin, athletic man who always wears a silk hat. On this occasion he took off his hat, raised his right leg well up into the air, bent his body, and, ducking his head under his leg, put his hat on it and then assumed a perpendicular position. It was a difficult feat. When the story was told to the President, he decided that any man who indulged in such undignified proceedings could not be a member of the Cabinet. So the story goes.

Regardless of the merits of the athletic performance, it might be that those of Lowry's friends who were most familiar with his financial habits would have agreed with the President's decision. As for Lowry's reaction, he said that he would not have accepted the appointment, and he may well have meant it. Harrison's Washington was probably pretty dull compared with Lowry's Minneapolis.

A Better Way to Move

TOM LOWRY'S FIRST LESSON IN HIGH FINANCE WAS IN THE ART OF borrowing money. His second lesson was in the nature of risk capital, and, like the first, it was learned from Boston men.

In the 1880s, New York was not yet the unquestioned financial center of the country, and Boston was the primary source of risk capital. Large fortunes had been accumulated by the masters of the sailing ships, and as they turned their eyes away from the sea, their money began to flow inland into a great variety of new ventures.

Lee Higginson and Company was the leading investment house in Boston and the highly respected headquarters of the Yankee capitalists. Their first notable success was in the Calumet Mines of northern Michigan, a source of tremendous profits. The same group backed J. Murray Forbes in the construction of the Chicago, Burlington and Quincy Railroad, and again the results were highly satisfactory.

The Burlington extended its tracks into St. Paul in 1885, and Charles Fairchild, an active partner of Lee Higginson and Company, traveled often to the Twin Cities. Like most imaginative visitors of those days, he became a good friend of Tom Lowry. During the latter part of 1886, Fairchild contracted to buy from Lowry a majority of the common stock of the St. Paul City Railway Company and the Minneapolis Street Railway Company for the account of Lee Higginson and Company and a group of its Boston clientele. The minutes of the stockholders' meetings began to carry

such distinguished names as Charles Francis Adams, John Quincy
Adams, Fred L. Ames, Godfrey and Louis Cabot, William Endi-
cott, J. Murray Forbes, N. P. Hallowell, Charles J. Paine, Lee
Saltonstall, Charles Thorndike, and many others. The price was
$45 per share for the Minneapolis stock and, probably, $25 per
share for the St. Paul shares. This transaction must have yielded
Lowry somewhat more than $1 million and doubtless provided
much of the wherewithal for his purchase of Soo Line stock and
other ventures of his. George B. Harris, general manager of the
Burlington Road, joined the board of the St. Paul City Railway
Company to represent the Boston stockholders.

The incentive for this purchase by the men of Boston is far from
clear. The horsecar companies had grown into substantial concerns
operating 250 cars over 80 miles of track with 500 employees and
1,500 horses and mules. But they were carrying an indebtedness of
more than $2 million, and after operating expenses and debt ser-
vice, there was seldom anything left for the stockholders. The Boston interest must have been sparked by the changes which were beginning to occur in the streetcar industry and by the profits which
were being predicted as a result of those changes.

The transfer of the controlling stock in the streetcar companies
from Lowry to the Boston syndicate was apparently unknown to
the public. Until his death, Lowry continued to give most of his
time and energy to the development of the streetcar system of which
he was generally regarded as the sole proprietor. And the scope of
his job was about to grow dramatically.

*   *   *

As urban population grew and as horsecar systems expanded, it
became more obvious that there had to be a better, more economical
way to move people. An adequate horse or mule, with a working
life of five years, cost $150, or $30 per year, plus 50 cents a day for
oats, hay, care, and housing. This brought the cost of one horse to

more than $200 per year, and it took 12 horses to keep one of the new larger horsecars moving through a 15-hour day, for a total power cost of $2,400 per car per year. There were very few horse-car operations earning more than their bare operating expenses, and certainly the Minneapolis and St. Paul systems were not among them. Since the riders could not afford to pay more than a five-cent fare (five cents was a lot to men earning a dollar a day), the answer had to be found in cheaper power.

Inventors scrambled to find such an answer, and the most obvious was the steam which powered the nation's railroads. The Remingtons made steam streetcars as early as 1872, and the Motor Line began running steam trains on Marquette Avenue in the summer of 1879. But people didn't like the noise and soot of steam engines running past their doors.

The cable car was the next effort to displace the horse, and it enjoyed the advantage of simplicity. The cable car operates on the same principle used by skiers grasping a moving rope. A long steel cable, driven by a stationary steam engine, travels in an endless loop at a fixed rate of speed under the pavement which carries the streetcar. Just as a skier grabs his traveling rope and moves uphill with it, the cable car grips the moving cable with a device thrust through the slot in a center rail beneath the streetcar. When the cable is gripped, the car moves at the eight miles an hour which is the cable's continuous speed; when the cable is released, the car can be braked to a stop.

As might be expected, the cable car was invented and first used in San Francisco, the hilliest city in the country, and it survives there to this day. But in other parts of the country, particularly where the climate is less moderate, the cable car was not so successful. The slot in the center rail, which had to be just the right size, was apt to shrink in cold weather and expand in hot weather. When it shrank, the gripping lever got stuck, and when it expanded, the wheels of passing drays and carriages were trapped.

The cable itself, which was often several miles long, caused other

A conductor applies the brakes as this cable car descends Selby Hill in St. Paul.

problems. Although the entire cable seldom parted, a broken strand could entangle the gripping mechanism, converting an orderly ride into a wild runaway. When this happened, the entire system had to be shut down—usually in the rush hour!

In spite of its shortcomings, the cable car was faster and cheaper to run than the horsecar. While the initial installation was much more expensive, the cost of operating a cable system was only half the cost of maintaining a fleet of horses. So by the early 1880s, cable cars were replacing horses in many American cities. But electricity was not far behind: the concepts of electric light and power had been simmering in the laboratories of the world for centuries, and the practical applications finally arrived.

The first arc lights in America were installed in Wanamaker's store in Philadelphia in 1878. Two years later, Thomas Edison invented a carbon filament lamp and then built a central power station in New York City to provide electricity for the lamps. At about the same time, a number of inventors began experimenting with electric motors. The imagination of the country turned to this new magical power, creating a flood of electrical inventions which inevitably answered the booming demand for urban transportation.

The pioneer builders of electric streetcars tried everything before finding a successful system. They fed electricity through the two running rails, but, if the voltage was high enough to move the car, it proved shocking to the public. The use of a third rail proved equally shocking, especially in a rainstorm. A man named Leo Daft first strung overhead wires in pairs and placed on them a device which transmitted electricity to the car, which in turn drew or trolled the device on wheels along the two overhead wires. This device became known as a "troller" and then a "trolley"; unfortunately, it often fell off the wires, landing on the roof of the car with a disconcerting crash. Another inventor, Charles Van Depoele, replaced Daft's two wires with one and pressed one wheel upwards against it by means of a pole and a spring mounted on the roof of the streetcar. But all of these early contraptions, while intriguing and promising, were so erratic in performance that they made little headway against the horsecars and the mushrooming cable car systems of the mid-1880s.

The breakthrough was furnished by Frank Sprague, whose many inventions, including the high-speed elevator, should have made his name much better known than it is. After a brief association with Thomas Edison, Sprague designed a superior electric motor and engineered it for streetcar use. A trolley pole, similar to Van Depoele's, collected direct current from an overhead wire, fed it through a controller to electric motors ingeniously mounted above the car's wheels, and completed the circuit by routing the used current back to generators along bonded steel tracks.

Sprague built his first streetcars and put them into operation in Richmond, Virginia, in February 1888. By summer of that year, the Richmond system was a proven success and was attracting streetcar magnates from every part of the country. The Sprague Electric Railway and Motor Company was overwhelmed by orders for its product and, in late 1889, was absorbed by the Edison General Electric Company. About the same time, Van Depoele's company was absorbed by the Thomson-Houston Company of Lynn, Massachusetts, and the race was on to remold our cities. During the next 10 years, the country's traction companies invested $2 billion in 15,000 miles of electrified track and 30,000 trolley cars, which were to change the life-style of millions of Americans.

Tom Lowry must have been one of the streetcar men who visited Richmond during the summer of 1888, when the Sprague cars were proving their superiority. The following letter shows how impressed he was:

Minneapolis, Minn. Sept. 21st, 1888

To the Honorable Mayor and Council
    of the City of Minneapolis.

Gentlemen:
    Electricity has within the past year or two been so widely discussed as a motive power for street railways, that it has interested not only street railway companies, but municipal authorities over the entire country. Our company has refused to make experiments, preferring to see its success clearly demonstrated before attempting its operation. This, it is claimed, has been accomplished in various cities in the United States. So confident are the promoters, that the Sprague Electric Railway and Motor Company has agreed to equip any or all the street railway lines in this city at its own expense, and guarantee the successful operation of the cars by electricity. Acting on this proposition, we have agreed with said company, —in case your honorable body grants the necessary permission, — to have the Hennepin and Lyndale Ave. line so equipped as a

test, with a view of adopting it on other lines in case it proves satisfactory to your honorable body and the travelling public. In the contract, the Sprague Electric Railway and Motor Company agree to "put said railway line in successful, practical, and satisfactory operation, and continue said operation from the first day of January, 1889, to the first day of June, 1889"; and also agree to "keep and maintain the same in practical, successful and satisfactory operation from January first, 1889, to June first, 1889, and hereby guarantees that said line of street railway shall be *capable* of operation, and *shall be operated to the satisfaction of the Street Railway Company and to the Public who patronize the same;* and the party of the first part is to assume all risk and responsibility for the successful and satisfactory operation of said line in all respects; and shall receive no payment of any sum whatever for anything furnished or done under this contract, unless said line operates efficiently, successfully and satisfactorily as aforesaid."

This seems a sufficient guaranty not only to the company, but to the public. With a view, therefore, of improving the street car service, we would ask your honorable body to grant the right to string the necessary overhead wires on Hennepin Avenue from Bridge Square to Lyndale Avenue; thence on Lyndale Avenue to Twenty-seventh Street; thence on Twenty-seventh Street to Dupont Avenue; thence on Dupont Avenue to the South line of City limits.

We would like early action on this, as by terms of the contract we are required to furnish the right-of-way within thirty days from September 14th, or the contract will be void. We are also anxious that the test of its successful operation should be made during the winter months.

We will retain our horses and present equipment so that in case of failure, the operation of the line will in no way be interrupted, as we will at once substitute the horses and operate the line as at present.

Respectfully,
Thomas Lowry.

In light of present-day knowledge, it's hard to understand why the council didn't promptly and enthusiastically accept this proposal. But in 1888 electricity inspired the same kind of doubts and fears which nuclear power does today. People foresaw mass electrocution of passengers, pedestrians, and animals. Mysterious electrical forces were thought likely to seep into water lines and sewers with unforeseeable results. So instead of approving the experimental line, the council referred the question to its Committee on Railways, setting the stage for the tumultuous events of 1889.

"Monopoly" vs. "Competition"

WHILE THE COMPANY AND THE COUNCIL WERE DEBATING THE complex questions of motive power, the general public was growing more restless and dissatisfied. Minneapolis was now a city of 150,000 people, and the glowing tales of cable cars and electric transportation in Chicago and New York made the old horsecars seem pretty shabby. The locomotives of the Motor Line, which was now operated by Lowry's company, were still spewing smoke and soot along Nicollet Avenue. And the company was still holding out against the practice, found in many cities, of permitting free transfer of passengers between connecting lines. There was increased muttering about the evils of monopoly and the need for competition in the streetcar business, and it was rumored that eastern capitalists were eyeing the Minneapolis market.

As the tide of public opinion began to run more heavily against him, Lowry decided that he had to act. If he couldn't get approval of the electric experiment, he would do the next best thing. On April 10, he announced his decision to build two cable lines. The first would replace the despised coal-burning Motor Line, and the second would replace the heavily traveled Washington Avenue horsecar line between Twentieth Avenue North and Cedar Avenue.

At the same time, Lowry posted in the car barns a notice which would be incredible today, and which, even in 1889, proved to be a shocker.

Minneapolis, Minn. April 10, 1889

To employees of the Minneapolis Street Railway Co.:

Owing to shrinkage of receipts and increased outlay, we are compelled to reduce expenses in all departments.

From and after April 14, the following will be the scale of wages:

Conductors and drivers on street cars	15 cents per hour
Stable men	$9 per week
Conductors on Motor Line	17 cents per hour
Engineers on Motor Line	25 cents per hour

Thomas Lowry, President

And Lowry opened the company's books to the press and summarized the 1888 operations as follows:

Earnings of the street railroad		$578,874
Earnings of the Motor Line		164,181
		$743,055
Operating expense of the street railroad	$472,623	
Operating expense of Motor Line	151,214	623,837
Operating profit		119,218
Interest on street railroad bonds	72,844	
Interest on Motor Line bonds	45,280	118,124
Profit		$ 1,094

In commenting on the figures, Lowry pointed out that the cost of extensions and improvements was not included in the expenses and that they had to be paid for by selling additional bonds. The new cable lines would also have to be paid for by selling bonds. The bonds could not be sold if the profits were not increased, and the only way to increase the profits was to reduce the men's wages. Lowry also stated that he himself had never drawn any salary from the company and had even paid the cost of travel on company business from his own pocket.

Unable to follow this reasoning, the men promptly struck. But after two weeks of partial service and occasional violence, the strike collapsed, and the men went back to work at the new wage scale, which represented a reduction of about 15 percent. The company won the strike, but the city's labor element, while still weak and unorganized, was now an outspoken enemy of the Lowry monopoly. Throughout the country "big business" was suffering increasing hostility. Edward Bellamy's *Looking Backward,* a vision of the socialist state, was selling a million copies, and the cause of the workingman was coming into fashion. Lowry won his point, but he acquired critics in the process.

A month later, on June 7, 1889, Lowry confirmed his cable line announcement by application to the city council. His formal proposal spelled out the conditions under which he was willing to replace the steam motors with cable cars running from the old Union Depot out Marquette and Nicollet to Thirty-First Street. But the council meeting on that evening was not the routine occasion that Lowry had expected.

The surprise was an application for a franchise for a new and extensive cable line system to compete with the Lowry monopoly. Attached to this application was a proposed ordinance specifying the streets on which the cable cars would run and defining a system which would serve the greater part of the city. Most of the new trackage would run on streets parallel to those used by the horsecars and would, in effect, duplicate the horsecar service.

The application was signed by two obscure real estate men, Robert J. Anderson and Walter P. Douglas, and it became known as the A and D franchise. The true nature and purpose of their application are still unknown. Douglas grew up in a respected Philadelphia family, moved to Chicago as a young man, and, in 1887, at age 31, came to Minneapolis to join Robert J. Anderson, who had just married his sister. Forming the real estate firm of Anderson, Douglas and Company, they lived in adjacent homes at 2401 and 2405 East Lake of the Isles Boulevard, and platted two small residential subdivisions in the same neighborhood. Douglas may have become associated with cable car magnate Charles Tyson Yerkes during his years in Chicago, but the only formal statement of their affiliations was vague. They told the council, "We have associated with us in the enterprise some of the wealthiest and most successful gentlemen in this line of business in the United States—gentlemen who are largely interested in the cable systems of Philadelphia, Chicago and Pittsburgh. It is the purpose of these gentlemen to proceed with all possible dispatch in the organization of a company to carry out the object indicated in this ordinance, to which company we propose to assign the rights thereby granted." While Anderson and Douglas were generally regarded as harbingers of a great modern public improvement, certain cynics thought they were simply seeking a franchise which, if granted, would be promptly peddled to Lowry for its nuisance value.

To city planners of today, the concept of two competitive systems of urban transportation would seem pure fantasy. But, in 1888, it was taken very seriously. In that day, a streetcar line was viewed as the rich prize it had proven to be in a few of the largest cities. Streetcar magnates were regarded as the millionaires which they were or at least pretended to be. The press used the Boston streetcar system as an example of a company growing fabulously rich on a five-cent fare when a two-cent fare would yield a fair profit. When Lowry said that his company was losing money and that he had never drawn a penny from its earnings, he was probably believed by very few members of the general public. They described his ownership of the company with that evil word *monopoly* and cited that worthy word *competition* as a desirable goal.

From July 7 until July 19, the issues were fiercely debated. William S. King, always a staunch friend of Lowry, wrote a lengthy letter to the editor of the *Tribune* stating the company's case. He pointed out that the city had granted Lowry's company an exclusive franchise, but only after including two conditions which would prevent it from becoming a burdensome monopoly. The first safeguard was limiting the fare to five cents, and the second was the council's power to order the company to build any line which the council declared reasonably necessary. King went on to say that the company had faithfully lived up to these provisions and was now offering to build cable lines only on the sections which could justify their cost. His final point was that a parallel system would prove to be folly because "where a street car track is not a public necessity, it is a public nuisance."

But most of the letters to the editor were in support of the competitive system. Some argued that the company had not built enough lines, but the most common complaint was the company's charging an additional nickel when a rider transferred from one line to another.

While the sponsorship of the Anderson and Douglas franchise did not play a prominent part in the debate, the following item appeared in the *Tribune* on July 19, 1889, one day before the council's decision. It makes interesting reading for those who recall Theodore Dreiser's *The Titan,* which portrays the Yerkes cable car operations in Chicago.

THE YERKES SYSTEM

How it has fastened its fangs on the people of Chicago
In an interview last night, H. E. Fletcher expressed himself very strongly on the evils of the Yerkes Cable System in Chicago. He said: "For two years I have been in a position to know just how the Yerkes Company was managing things in Chicago, and have arrived at the conclusion that you don't want anything of that sort here. The whole scheme of the company has been in the nature of a swindle, and now the people of Chicago have it on their hands and can't get rid of it. Here is a statement from a correspondent of mine in Chicago. He is well informed on the matter.

" 'Anyone who has taken any of the Chicago papers excepting the Chicago Times, which has been bought and paid for by these parties, can hardly fail to have observed the almost daily comments of the press in execration of their measures, their methods and their service. They have been brutal,

conscienceless and wholly shameless in everything they have
done or attempted to do. Their interests here are entrusted to
the management and keeping of a convicted criminal. The
bribery of public officers of all grades is carried on as system-
atically and almost as openly as the purchase of horse food. It
is doubtless by means of bribery that they expect to break into
Minneapolis and unless you can bar the door of your common
council against them by means of an overwhelming public
opinion, they will get there. They are a bad set. Wholly bad.
Whatever their promises they will give you nothing but bad
fruit for what they get from you. They will use the franchise,
if you give them one, simply as a basis to sell pictures. You
will get no service, no value received.' "

While the *Tribune* seemed to try to present both sides of the argu-
ment, the *Journal* was outspoken in its approval of the Anderson
and Douglas proposal. An evening paper selling for two cents, the
Journal was overtaking the circulation of the established *Tribune,* a
morning paper selling for five cents. Flogging the hide of a reputed
millionaire and monopolist such as Tom Lowry was apparently a
useful ingredient in its bid for circulation, and the paper went all
out in its advocacy of competition in the transportation business.
Reading the accounts of the contest carried by the *Tribune* and the
Journal, one can imagine Lowry as a public-spirited man working
his heart out for the advancement of the city, or, on the other hand,
as a bloated plutocrat and arch-villain. But even the *Journal* spoke
of Tom Lowry's "irresistible way" of handling himself in a difficult position.

As the Committee on Railways was drafting its report to the
council and as the day of decision approached, both sides undoubtedly sought every possible means of influencing the numerous
aldermen. As the city had grown and formed new wards, the council had increased from 12 to the unwieldy number of 39—3 members from each of the 13 wards, as compared with 1 from each ward
today. Atwater's history of Minneapolis, published in 1893, makes
the following comments on the evolution of the governing body:

It is interesting to observe the change which has gradually been going on during the last fifteen or twenty years in the personnel of the legislative department of the city. For several years, in the early history of the city, the compensation of the Aldermen was hardly more than nominal. — There was then no inducement to seek the office for the salary attached to it. And yet the ablest businessmen, and those representing the largest interests, were willing to accept the office. [Atwater was referring to such men as George Brackett, Hugh Harrison, C. B. Heffelfinger, Dorilus Morrison, and C. M. Loring.] By the act of incorporation of the City of Minneapolis, the Council was to consist of twelve members. With the growth of the city, the number was subsequently increased until, at the present time, the Council consists of thirty-nine members, and the salary of an Alderman is $750. Meantime, few if any men representing the largest tax payers and business interests of the city are found willing to accept the office of Alderman. The raising of salaries has not resulted in securing better representative men, nor has the increase in numbers served to secure more useful and conservative legislation.

The 1890 city directory gives the following picture of the occupations of the 39 aldermen. For six, no occupation was listed; eight were involved in real estate and loans; nine were members of contracting and building trades; three were lawyers; four worked in the saddlery and livery; one was a physician; one was an undertaker; one was a saloon keeper; and six were listed under "miscellaneous trades."

The supporters of Anderson and Douglas organized public meetings in several wards, demanded their alderman's presence, and hurled every sort of insinuation at those who wouldn't promise to vote their way. "You've been bought" was the most common charge, but who bought whom (if anyone) was by no means clear. The press accounts of these meetings bear a striking likeness to the Yerkes methods in Chicago as portrayed by Dreiser.

The streetcar company retaliated by collecting petitions against the Anderson and Douglas franchise from the citizens who lived on the streets which would carry the Anderson and Douglas cable cars if the franchise were granted.

Charges and countercharges grew in warmth. The *Journal* charged that Lowry owned the *Tribune,* and the *Tribune's* editor, Blethen, replied that he personally owned every share of the paper's stock.

On July 18, the Committee on Railways met and adopted, by a vote of six to two, a report which came down squarely in favor of Lowry's company. Using the same reasoning as in King's letter, the report pointed out the absurdities which would result from two competing systems and recommended that the existing company be given the first opportunity to provide the cable lines which everyone wanted and the free transfers between connecting lines which everyone had come to expect.

The report went on to specify the streets for three cable lines to be built by the company, together with completion dates. Finally, the committee made a provision for an experimental electric line to be chosen at a later date. The obvious inconsistency between ordering three extensive cable lines and at the same time proposing an experimental electric line drew no comment whatever. One can only surmise that, in July of 1889, the possibilities of an electric system, despite its success in Richmond, were outweighed by the pressure of public opinion for an immediate improvement over the horsecar by means of the cable system, which was still regarded as the safer path of progress.

The council met the next evening, July 19, to act on the committee's report, and the council chamber was jammed with the friends of competition and the enemies of monopoly. After lengthy debate, the roll was called. Each vote for Anderson and Douglas was cheered and each vote for Lowry was hissed and booed.

The *Journal's* vitriolic report of the outcome (July 20) follows:

> Alderman Frederick Brueshaber, the proprietor of a saloon at 25th Avenue Northeast, sat in the Council Chamber last night quietly puffing a cigar. It was midnight of the largest

and most important meeting that the City Council ever had. The Council Chamber was packed to suffocation. Great beads of sweat stood on Clerk Haney's manly brow and trickled down upon his shirt collar. He was calling the names of the Aldermen on the vote that was to decide the most important measure to the interested parties and the people that ever has and perhaps ever will come before a body of the people's representatives in Minneapolis. The excitement was intense. People who had stood patiently for hours while the routine business of the Council was being disposed of and all the preliminaries of the great battle were being arranged listened as each name was called, watching as the balance swung back and forth, for and against the Anderson and Douglas franchise. At last the list was completed. A great shout went up. The people had won by 20 votes to 19, and monopoly was defeated.

But no! Fortune in mere wanton frivolity last night raised the cup of victory to the lips of the people only to dash it, at the last moment, from their lips.

Just before the vote was announced, Alderman Brueshaber, faintly and between the puffs of his cigar, rose and ejaculated: "Mr. President, I change my vote to no."

By this one feebly expressed sentence, the hopes of threefourths of the people that the Council represents were for the nonce destroyed.

A chorus of hisses arose from the crowd and expressions of disgust overspread the faces of those present.

A saloonkeeper, weak of will and uncertain of his own mind, had suddenly become a veritable reigning monarch. He held the interests of the people with his cigar between his two fingers. Then wantonly, almost as if it was a matter of indifference, he tossed his vote on the side of the people, then finally on the side of monopoly.

Fortunately, the business community apparently did not share the *Journal*'s viewpoint. As part of its conclusion, the council ordered the company to post a $225,000 bond as a guaranty of performance. In those days, such bonds were not sold by insurance companies. They took the form of guaranties by individuals who, upon signing them, became personally liable in case of default. In addition to Lowry, the following men signed the $225,000 bond:

M. B. Koon	Charles A. Pillsbury
C. G. Goodrich	A. H. Linton
Henry F. Brown	H. G. Harrison
T. B. Walker	E. W. Herrick
R. B. Langdon	George R. Newell
Clinton Morrison	C. H. Pettit
C. M. Loring	Samuel C. Gale
H. E. Fletcher	D. M. Clough
O. C. Merriman	Samuel Hill

While Lowry had won the contest, the first consequence of the victory was a dead loss. In order to meet the council's completion dates, the cable lines had to be commenced immediately, and large quantities of cable equipment were ordered, delivered, and stacked along the proposed lines at a reported cost of $300,000. But in less than 60 days, on September 14, 1889, the council authorized an experimental electric line similar to that which Lowry had requested a year earlier. The route finally approved was to run from First Avenue South and Third Street on out Fourth Avenue to Thirty-Fourth Street South.

While the cable equipment lay unused, the Electric Line was rushed to completion. The old, light horsecar rails with their "narrow gauge" of 3 feet 6 inches were torn up and replaced by heavier rails of "standard gauge," 4 feet 8½ inches apart. Eight of the newest and largest horsecars were rebuilt by removing their bodies from the old trucks and placing them upon heavy four-wheel trucks designed to receive the electric motors. The electricity was furnished by a steam engine and an electric generator located in the old Pray Manufacturing Company building on First Street and Fifth Avenue South. Poles were erected on each side of the street to support the span wires which carried the electrified trolley wires above the tracks. The work was done with such determination that the first electric streetcars were placed in service at 4:00 P.M. on the

Minneapolis' first electric streetcar. It began service on December 24, 1889.

day before Christmas, only 100 days after the council's authority was received. On December 25, 1889, the *Tribune* reported:

IT'S OPEN

The Fourth Avenue Electric Line in Complete Operation

At exactly 4 o'clock yesterday afternoon, 8 new electric cars on the 4th Avenue Line began to move from 2nd Ave. South on 3rd St. for the first time for the transportation of the public. The drivers and conductors, with long ulster coats, buttoned all the way with brass buttons, filled out their breasts, looked straight ahead and felt even more dignified than the passengers aboard, who looked out upon their friends standing upon the pavement. Ding, ding, ding, round the corner and straight out 4th Avenue the cars swept majestically, while the hundreds of onlookers pronounced them just the thing as they ran along as smooth as is possible to be conceived. . . .

The Fourth Avenue Line won immediate and unanimous approval. The many doubters, who had predicted every sort of disaster, grew silent. On January 17, 1890, after three weeks of the new service, the city council directed the company to substitute electric street railways, similar to that on Fourth Avenue, for the three cable lines previously ordered and on any other horsecar lines it might choose. Electricity was finally in. The cable equipment was sold for scrap.

The transition from horse to electric power, which had been so confusing in Minneapolis, was no more orderly in St. Paul.

While not as mountainous as the land in San Francisco, the bluff overlooking St. Paul's business district offered an obvious challenge to the cable car. The first cable line in Minnesota was built in 1887 by Lowry's St. Paul City Railway Company, from Broadway westward on Fourth and Third Streets up the bluff and out Selby Avenue to St. Albans Street. A second cable line, of about the same length, was finished in June 1889, and ran from Wabasha out Seventh Street to Duluth Avenue.

At about the same time, John Ireland, archbishop of the Roman Catholic archdiocese of Minneapolis and St. Paul, proposed the construction of electric lines which would link downtown St. Paul with a new real estate development taking shape around a tract of land owned by the Archdiocese and St. Thomas Seminary.

In June, 1889, Archbishop Ireland, a real estate developer named Thomas Cochrane, and Lowry's St. Paul City Railway Company entered into an agreement under which the railway company, in return for a $250,000 bonus, would construct and operate two electric lines. The first was to run from Wabasha and Seventh out Oakland and Grand Avenues to Cleveland, where a terminal was located two blocks from the St. Thomas Seminary; the second would run on Fourth Street from Wabasha to Seventh Street and on out Seventh to Randolph and along Randolph to Cleveland.

In pursuance of this agreement, the St. Paul City Railway Company asked the St. Paul City Council for authority to proceed with the construction of the first two lines and also for the right to electrify its horsecar lines. By the time that the necessary ordinance had been prepared, several other individuals and corporations had applied for franchises to build competing and conflicting lines on the streets of St. Paul, and, as in Minneapolis, the council was faced

The first electric streetcar operated in St. Paul. This picture, taken on February 22, 1890, shows Tom Lowry *(right)* and Archbishop John Ireland *(second from right)* in the front seat.

with the responsibility of choosing between applicants. After much agitation and discussion, Lowry asked the St. Paul Chamber of Commerce to appoint a committee to confer with the council's committee in an effort to arrive at a joint recommendation. After many meetings, both public and private, the joint committee recommended that Lowry's St. Paul City Railway Company be granted the right to operate all of its lines by cable, electric, pneumatic, or gas power, at the option of the company. The council unanimously accepted the recommendation by resolution of September 19, 1889, which was only five days after the approval of the first electric line by the Minneapolis council.

Early in 1890, as the frost left the ground, work began in earnest. A construction crew of 1,200 men in Minneapolis and 1,200 in St. Paul undertook the enormous job of building a brand new transportation system for both cities. The old tracks were relaid on adjacent streets to provide temporary horsecar service, and the new

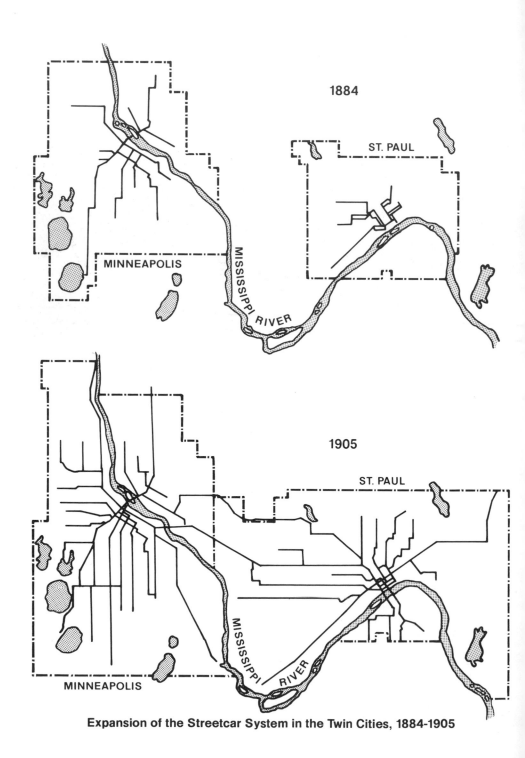

1884

ST. PAUL

MINNEAPOLIS

MISSISSIPPI RIVER

1905

ST. PAUL

MINNEAPOLIS

MISSISSIPPI RIVER

Expansion of the Streetcar System in the Twin Cities, 1884-1905

heavy standard-gauge tracks went down. Trolley wires were strung to carry the electricity and were supported by poles in the centers of the streets. In Minneapolis two new powerhouses were built at Third Avenue North and Second Street and at Nicollet and Thirty-First Street, housing boiler and steam engines and 26 Edison generators with a total capacity of 3,600 horsepower. A St. Paul powerhouse, with another 16 Edison generators, was built on Hill Street near Kellogg Boulevard to propel the cars on the east side of the river. As each new line was completed, the horses were sold and new electric cars were placed in service. While the oldest horsecars were scrapped, the newer ones were converted to electrified streetcars. Some of the horsecars were converted to trailers that were pulled by the electrified streetcars; these provided an economic means of increasing the capacity of the streetcars.

Among the new lines built was the Interurban, completed on December 9, 1890, linking the business districts of the two cities via Washington and University Avenues. When the job was substantially complete, at the close of 1891, less than four years after Sprague's success in Richmond, the last horsecar was scrapped, and the Twin Cities could claim a system of urban transportation which was, physically, as good as or better than any other in the country. But financially, the system was not nearly as impressive.

Financing the Streetcar Companies

AFTER THE STREETCAR COMPANIES HAD WON THEIR BATTLE IN THE councils of the two cities, they found themselves in a curious financial position. They now had the authority to build a great transportation system, but they had no money. They owed more than $4 million, which had been spent on the old system. And the old system, with the possible exception of the St. Paul cable lines, had just been declared obsolete and worthless. Before signing contracts for new construction and equipment estimated to cost at least $6 million, the companies understandably thought it would be prudent to know where the money was coming from.

Many of the nation's streetcar companies were finding themselves in a similar position. Almost from necessity, various means of financial assistance were being offered by the manufacturers of the electrical equipment used in the new systems. The largest of these concerns was the Edison General Electric Company, which had recently absorbed the Sprague Electric Railway and Motor Company.

Henry Villard and a cohort of German capitalists had put together and controlled the Edison General Electric Company. This was the same Villard who, some years earlier, had taken over the Northern Pacific Railroad Company and completed the first unbroken railway between the Twin Cities and the Pacific Coast. Lowry, along with everyone else in the Twin Cities, could remember the gala days in September 1883, when Villard and his Ger-

Henry Villard, a capitalist who signed a contract to finance Lowry's new system

man friends were received in St. Paul and feted as heroes under the triumphal Villard Arches, which had been erected for that occasion. And when the Villard party had then entrained for the ceremonial trip to Puget Sound, Lowry had gone along as one of Villard's guests. So Lowry and Villard were doubtless well acquainted.

Shortly after the new electric streetcar system had been authorized by the two city councils and before the contracts were let, Lowry went to New York to confer with Villard. Charles Fairchild, of Lee Higginson and Company, joined the discussion, and the negotiations went on for several weeks. In March 1890, Henry Villard signed a contract agreeing to provide all of the money required to build and equip Lowry's new system. While there is no record of the details of this agreement, both Lowry and Fairchild accepted it as an unconditional guaranty of the funds, and in March 1890, nobody questioned the goodness of a Villard commitment. On March 28, 1890, the boards of the two streetcar companies authorized the execution of construction contracts and the purchase of 180 double electric motors from Villard's Sprague Electric

The Villard Arches in St. Paul were erected to celebrate the completion of the first unbroken railway between the Twin Cities and the Pacific Coast.

Railway and Motor Company. With the financing apparently concluded and the contracts let, Lowry took a European vacation.

The subsequent misfortune was probably due to factors beyond
Villard's control, but the results were nonetheless painful. During
that chaotic summer of 1890, the United States Congress on July
14 passed the Sherman Silver Purchase Act, which profoundly
shook the world's confidence in the American dollar. Then, on November 20, the dominant London banking house of Baring Brothers failed, and days later, the New York firm of Decker, Howell
and Company, which was known as Villard's brokerage firm, was
declared bankrupt. Villard, though his credit was badly shaken, expressed confidence in his ability to fulfill his obligation to the Twin
City Lines. But by the year's end, it became clear that he couldn't,
and Lowry would have to look elsewhere for funds to pay the bills,
which were now pouring in from every direction.

Fortunately, Tom Lowry was well qualified for this difficult job.
During the past 10 years, he had made himself one of the best-
known and best-liked "westerners" on Wall Street. An article in
the *Minneapolis Tribune* of February 4, 1909, written by a New
York reporter named R. W. Vincent and published after Lowry's
death, describes his visits to the financial capital of the country.

> Mr. Lowry held miniature but practically continuous recep-
> tions on his New York trips from the time he emerged from
> his room at the hotel (it was usually the Holland House) in
> the morning until he returned there late at night. No sooner
> did he appear in the halls, in the corridors, the livingrooms, on
> the street or the elevated trains than someone approached him
> with, "How do you do Mr. Lowry," or "Tom, old fellow,
> glad to see you." The tall and handsome Westerner always
> had an unfailing supply of cordiality to dispense, and invari-
> ably left his friends in better humor than he found them.
>
> Mr. Lowry transacted about as much business on the street
> as he did in bankers' and brokers' offices. When he chanced to
> meet a friend whom he thought should have some Twin City
> or Soo securities, Mr. Lowry, after extending a characteristi-

cally cordial greeting and telling one of his equally characteristic and side-splitting stories, proceeded to tell the man that
he should not rest easy until he had bought himself a few hun-
dred shares of Twin City or Soo Line stock or a few thousand
bonds of one or both companies. Mr. Lowry had the man
hypnotized, as it were, and the latter straightaway acted upon
the genial president's advice.

And so it went all day long and every day while Mr.
Lowry was in town. Extreme optimism and good stories
paved the way for a ready market for all the securities he had
to offer. More seriously, however, New York financiers had
absolute confidence in him, and when he came to town bub-
bling over with glowing reports of rapidly increasing traffic on
the Twin City lines and of excellent crops in the territory covered by the Soo system, his friends were ready to take his
bonds and stocks, and to hand him over the necessary cash to
supply his companies with the much needed increased facilities. In view of these facts, it is easy to understand how Mr.
Lowry had no difficulty in selling bonds when bankers were
trying in vain to find a market for the issues of much larger
railroad propositions than those which Mr. Lowry headed.

One evening the New York representative of the Tribune
received a dispatch directing him to see Mr. Lowry at his hotel that night without fail with respect to an important matter
in the affairs of the Twin City Rapid Transit Company. The
reporter arrived at the hotel just in time to see Mr. Lowry,
with a party of ladies, passing through the main corridor to
take carriages for the theatre. In sheer desperation, the news-
paperman approached Mr. Lowry, at that seemingly inoppor-
tune moment, for an interview. Greatly to the fellow's surprise (for he was not well acquainted with Mr. Lowry at that
time), the latter received him with extreme cordiality and actually asked his ladies to wait while he answered the questions
of the reporter. Few men of far less importance in the world of
affairs would have done this and with the extreme gracious-
ness which Mr. Lowry displayed.

But he was "Tom Lowry," the genial, good-hearted,
whole-hearted fellow and perfect gentleman, and he could not
have done otherwise if he had tried.

When Villard's commitment fell through, and the urgent need arose for other sources of capital, Lowry was doubtless the ideal man for the job. But even with his experience and reservoir of goodwill on Wall Street, the obstacles were formidable. Money was tight and bankers were already overcommitted. The Sherman Silver Act and the Baring Brothers' failure had temporarily dried up the flow of British capital which had been such an important factor in the expansion of American industry.

The original plan had called for raising about $5,800,000 through the sale of bonds of the two companies. In January 1891, there remained unsold about $1 million in bonds of the Minneapolis company and about $1.5 million in bonds of the St. Paul company. Villard's contract had probably called for his buying these securities himself or placing them in one of his holding companies. But Villard was no longer in a position to do either.

Fairchild, representing the Boston stockholders, again joined Lowry in New York, and it took them almost six months to raise the money. Their two best prospects were J. Kennedy Tod and Jacob Schiff.

Tod must have been one of the ablest young bankers on Wall Street. In 1891, at 39, he had taken over his uncle's influential banking house and was a director of about 15 important corporations, including the Great Northern Railroad and the influential Central Trust Company of New York. An intellectual, he authored a book entitled *The XYZ of Money* and inscribed a copy "To Thomas Lowry Esq. because he has abundant 'capital' and never has any 'money.'"

Schiff headed the powerful house of Kuhn, Loeb and Company, the only real rival of J. P. Morgan. Lowry used to tell the story of the day he sold some bonds to Schiff and was then taken to the banker's mansion for lunch. Schiff, who must have been known for thriftiness, was accustomed to ask a blessing before his meals, and as he expressed gratitude for "that which we are about to receive," Lowry muttered under his breath, "at 65 cents on the dollar."

The Minneapolis bonds were relatively easy to sell. But the St. Paul bonds were very sticky. The St. Paul cable lines, built in 1887 and 1888, were planned to cost $600,000 but actually had run to almost $1 million. To make matters worse, the cable cars were plagued with accidents and breakdowns. In addition, St. Paul was, for various reasons, not nearly so good a streetcar town as Minneapolis, and the St. Paul earnings had lagged from the start.

Tod and Schiff were willing to buy the St. Paul bonds if Lowry could find one other qualified banker to take part of them. Morton, Bliss and Company almost agreed but didn't. Hamilton Twombly made a trip to St. Paul, returned to New York, and declined. The unsold bonds still amounted to $1,750,000, and Lowry was getting desperate.

It was J. Kennedy Tod who devised a method of making the St. Paul bonds more palatable by placing the credit of the Minneapolis company behind them. Tod proposed the formation of a new holding company which would acquire all the stock of both streetcar companies and which would then guaranty the St. Paul bonds. On June 3, 1891, the Twin City Rapid Transit Company was organized for this purpose. J. Kennedy Tod and Company and Kuhn, Loeb and Company finally bought the St. Paul bonds, but even with the holding company's guaranty, they exacted a further concession. About 20 percent of the common stock of the two streetcar companies was delivered to the bankers, together with an attractive purchase option. Apparently half of this stock was put up by the Boston stockholders and the other half by Lowry. The disaster had been narrowly averted, but at a considerable sacrifice.

Lowry wrote to Higginson: "Am a *little* weary. I feel something like the old lady who was the mother of 14 children. She said,

> It seems to me that when I die,
> Before I join the blest,
> I'd like just for a little while,
> To lie in my grave and rest."

Lowry's experiences on Wall Street gave rise to many stories, of which the *Bellman,* a Minneapolis magazine, wrote in its February 13, 1909, issue: "None of them eclipses the famous incident when, as he stood with Charles Fairchild in Wall Street wondering how he should begin to raise the million or so which at that moment he had to have for his immediate needs, a beggar woman asked alms of him. 'Yes, yes,' he said as he handed her a quarter, 'but you go and work that side of the street; I'm working this side.' "

Another story concerns Lowry's first visit to the prestigious office of J. Pierpont Morgan, who is said to have greeted him with a stern look and this comment: "Young man, I am not accustomed to doing business with anyone who has whiskey on his breath—especially at ten o'clock in the morning!" To which Lowry supposedly replied: "Mr. Morgan, I beg your pardon, but to tell you the truth, it never occurred to me that I could face a man of your prominence without just a touch of Irish courage." The two men became good friends.

Lowry's sense of humor must have saved him time and time again, not only from financial ruin but also from the despair which overcomes many men in hopeless situations. Somehow Tom Lowry could always see the humorous, or sometimes ridiculous, side of his dilemma. Friends remembered seeing him, at the very moment of a bitter disappointment, burst into laughter. And when things went right, the laughter made success even more enjoyable.

Celebration!

THOSE HECTIC SIX MONTHS IN NEW YORK WERE FOLLOWED BY A year or so of relatively smooth sailing. By the close of 1891, the transformation of the streetcar system was close to completion. The narrow-gauge iron rails of the horsecar era had been taken up and replaced with 210 miles of heavy steel track. There were two electric power stations in Minneapolis and one in St. Paul with a total of 42 electric generators. More than 400 electric streetcars were carrying over 100,000 passengers per day at speeds up to 25 miles per hour. The citizens were convinced that they had the finest transportation system in the world; perhaps they did.

In the ebullient spirit of those days, a celebration was proposed. On January 11, 1892, a banquet was convened at the West Hotel which was reminiscent of the occasion which marked the hotel's completion. But this gathering was in honor of Tom Lowry and the completion of his transportation system. Again the banquet was underwritten and attended by the leading businessmen of Minneapolis and St. Paul, some 350 in number. Governor Merriam and Archbishop Ireland, together with Lowry, greeted the guests and ushered them to the long, place-carded tables which had seated a similar group seven years earlier. The menu, too, was similar, with seven courses and five wines. Professor Danz and his Harmonia Hall Orchestra were on hand to provide a wide assortment of waltzes, gavottes, polkas, and galops.

Few men are privileged to enjoy such a triumphal occasion. The testimonial speeches rolled on, replete with every ornate platitude of the day. They were recorded in the *Minneapolis Tribune* of January 12, 1892.

Archbishop Ireland spoke at length of the extent and quality of the new transit system:

> We have the best system of electric roads in the country. No city approaches us in excellence of equipment, in the application of the latest developments of science, in the perfection of all details. Whatever its size, no one city in America has so many miles of electric line as Minneapolis and St. Paul. Indeed, if I am to credit an article in the December number of the Cosmopolitan Review, we have today in our two cities an electric mileage nearly equal to that in all other American cities united. No large city, outside of our own two, has as yet been able to discard its horse cars. We lead America; we lead the world. Strong words, but absolutely true!

As Tom Lowry listened to words like these repeated by the speakers of the evening, he must have been deeply pleased, but he also must have been reminded of the mistakes of those hectic days and the problems yet to be solved. The Sprague electric motors were defective and would have to be rebuilt. The St. Paul Cable Lines were still plagued by accidents and breakdowns and would have to be replaced. And the financing, which had finally been obtained, had proven insufficient to pay for the completed job. There was $2 million in floating debt, and the banks were beginning to press.

One portion of Ireland's speech must have struck Lowry as truly ironic. It was only two years ago that he was being charged with the evils of monopoly, but now monopoly was viewed as a public blessing.

"In other places," Ireland said, "a street car company transfers, as ours does, its passengers from one of its lines to another. But in other places, there are two or more separate companies, and there is no transfer from the territory of one to that of another. Here *one* company reigns, and its travelers, one fare paid, are lords and masters of all they survey."

Of the seven speakers at the banquet, ex-Senator Pierce must have given the most pleasing oration. Commenting on Lowry's "spirit of a boy and that perfect simplicity which is such a prominent trait in his character," Pierce went on to say:

> Great wealth buys great power, and often great pride and arrogance. We all know how that is ourselves. We know how hard it is to be simple since we got to be rich. But it is not hard for him. He is the same Tom, to rich and poor, high and low alike, as he was twenty or twenty-five years ago when he hustled through the streets of Minneapolis hunting for a victim on whom he could experiment as an unfledged lawyer. I don't know that he deserves much credit for this, for I hardly think he can help it.
>
> Let me close by saying here's to our guest! Big-hearted, broad-shouldered, long-legged, long-headed Tom.
>
> Boast as we may of our sunny skies and our incomparable climate, we have to admit that in the Northwest it is always Lowry.

Lowry's own comments were rather brief. After thanking the sponsors and telling a humorous story, he took the opportunity to plead once more for greater unity and better cooperation between the two cities:

> We must draw capital and people from the outside, and we must unite with it our capital and efforts in order to build up a great city. We must all do our full share. Occasionally, we shall meet with a rebuff, but we must be as our friend, Mr. Wheelock, the editor of the Pioneer Press says. You must learn to
>
> > Spur up your virtue and put a check rein on your pride.
> > And carry a gentleman's manners beneath a rhinoceros hide.

While this banquet was tendered ostensibly to me, let us all consider ourselves equal partners. Consider this a new association formed tonight to advance every material element that tends to build up a great city. Let us form an association, and as individuals do our work in both capacities with cheerfulness, courage and vim. Let our motto be, "No Minneapolis, no St. Paul, but one great city." Let it be no Minneapolis and no St. Paul, but one great city that in the year 1900 will roll up by an honest count 1,000,000 people.

Few men have been accorded the honor Tom Lowry enjoyed on that evening. Forty-nine years old, at the height of his abilities and prestige, he must have seemed among the most fortunate of men. But his head never seemed to be turned by success. Perhaps his problems and disappointments always sufficiently balanced the most extravagant praise. He wrote the following letter to a friend just a month after the testimonial dinner:

James Goldsbury, Esq., City.

Dear Mr. Goldsbury:—
 Your very welcome letter of the 20th ult. reached me in New York and I intended acknowledging it at once, but in the press of business neglected—as we often do—that sacred duty.
 I say "sacred duty" because it can not be less when a friend and neighbor takes the pains to voluntarily give me such a testimonial as your letter contains. I do not merit all the good things said of me, nor do I deserve all the criticisms heaped upon me. But when you strike an average I guess it won't be far from right. After all, the average is what "counts," and is the standard by which one is judged. Do not be uneasy about me becoming "sour," for I could not if I tried.
 I am always happy, contented, and thankful to both my friends and enemies; to the former for their kind words and good offices, and to the latter for the lesson they teach me— i.e., that one can do more good to others, enjoy to a greater extent the blessings of life, and contribute to his own health and capabilities more in one minute by forgiving and loving his

A portrait of Tom Lowry at age 49

enemies, than by hating them for a whole lifetime.

I intend to make a "good time" for my friends, have a "good time" myself and lend a helping hand to my enemies whenever opportunity offers and circumstances permit.

Again thanking you, I am,

Sincerely yours,
Tom Lowry

This letter calls to mind a phrase which Lowry used in his response at the dinner: "a gentleman's manners beneath a rhinoceros hide." He would need them both in the years that lay immediately ahead.

Keeping Afloat

HORACE B. HUDSON, IN *A HALF CENTURY OF MINNEAPOLIS,* WROTE: "To Minneapolis, the shock of the financial disaster of 1893 came almost as a complete surprise. It had seemed that prosperity was a thing which belonged to Minneapolis as a right; in many people's minds, continued growth and constant advance in values of property and volume of business were assured."

A little hindsight clearly reveals that the panic of 1893 should have come as no surprise. While the 1880s had been marked by dramatic inventions and rapid expansion in most industries, the economy was being sapped by a monetary deflation which seemed to go largely unobserved. As a result of protective tariffs on imports enacted in 1884, the federal government was suffering from an embarrassment of riches. In 1885, federal receipts of $323 million exceeded expenditures by $63 million, which was, as a matter of course, used to reduce the federal debt. During the next four years, the debt was reduced by an additional $367 million, and the retirement of U.S. bonds, which were the basis for bank-issued currency, automatically reduced the amount of money in circulation. In the resulting deflation, prices, and then wages, began to fall. When Lowry announced a reduction in wage rates in the summer of 1889, he was following a pattern being forced on many businesses by shrinkage of the money supply.

When Washington finally woke up to what was happening, the principal remedy it chose was the unfortunate passage of the Sherman Silver Purchase Act, which was expected to increase the currency in circulation but which served only to shake the world's confidence in the currency already in use. Followed closely by the Baring Brothers failure, the stage was set for the gradual economic slide which culminated in the panic of 1893.

During the early months of 1893, Minneapolitans read of the convulsions in the eastern money markets and the erosion of values on the New York Stock Exchange. It was in May that the panic became a local reality with the bankruptcy of Louis Menage and his Guaranty Loan Company.

Tom Lowry was supposedly in New York when the bad news about the Guaranty Loan Company arrived. J. Kennedy Tod was giving a large luncheon in honor of a London banker, and, after several of the guests had asked him about the Guaranty Loan rumors, he tapped his water glass for attention and asked Lowry if he had any information on the subject. Lowry replied:

> Your question reminds me of an incident which occurred recently on the Broadway Limited. A number of gentlemen had retired to the Club Car and as they were smoking their after-dinner cigars, one of them was seen to sniff the air, frown and leave the car. Then a second and a third man followed him and soon there was only one man left. After a few minutes, the Pullman Conductor appeared, sniffed the air and approached the remaining occupant to inquire: "Sir, I've had complaints about an offensive odor in this car. Can you tell me anything about it?" "Well, yes, I can," the gentleman replied. "I regret to say that I'm sitting right in the middle of it."

The cause of the Menage disaster can be traced back to the affairs of Colonel William S. King. Philo Remington foreclosed his mortgage on King's 1,400-acre Lyndale Farm and bought up King's bankrupt estate in 1878; in 1882, Remington sold the Lyndale Farm to Louis Menage, who, in the population boom of the early eighties, converted it into a very successful residential development. In 1884, King filed a lawsuit against Remington in which he contended that he had deeded the property to Remington in trust as security for the repayment of a loan; that the loan had now been paid in full from the sale of property; that King's equity had never been extinguished; and that the balance of the property, in excess of the amount used to repay Remington's loan, should be returned to King. The district court and then the Minnesota Supreme Court upheld King's contention. Furthermore, the courts held that Menage, rather than being an "innocent buyer," was a partner of Remington. And Menage was ordered to turn over to King property and mortgages valued at about $2 million, the rough equivalent of $20 million in today's currency.

While Menage's formal bankruptcy did not occur until May 1893, it seems he had actually been insolvent ever since his settlement with Colonel King in 1886. When the crash came, Menage made a sudden move to Guatemala City, where he could block his extradition. In January 1895, he wrote a lengthy letter, printed in the February 23, 1895, issue of the *Minneapolis Times,* in which he sought to vindicate himself and obtain immunity from prosecution. His letter portrays a man who had spent seven years inflating his enterprises in a vain effort to regain the $2 million which he had lost in the King-Remington lawsuit. An excerpt from his letter reads: "With the belief that a building of its own would be a great benefit in extending the company's connections, the matter was laid before Mr. Lowry with the result that the capital was increased, new interest taken in the company by Minneapolis men, the lot purchased of Honorable W. D. Washburn for about $210,000 and the building commenced."

Apparently Tom Lowry had been no more able to reject the concept of Minneapolis' first "skyscraper" than the West Hotel or any of the other proposals for the advancement of the city. And the Guaranty building was the first of several which came home to haunt him during the grim years of 1893 through 1897. As a vice-president and heavy stockholder in Menage's companies, he was indeed "sitting right in the middle of it."

Another such enterprise was the Minneapolis Stockyards and Packing Company. Organized in 1887, this company was struggling with the problems common to most newly launched ventures when it was sunk by the financial storm of 1893. William Henry Eustis was secretary-treasurer of the stockyards. In his autobiography, he recalls:

> One night the group of stockholders in this stockyards venture gathered at the office of Mr. Lowry, who always found the silver lining regardless of the depth of the clouds. And there were clouds aplenty that night. The enterprise had blown up, the obligations were genuine and the money market was a thing tighter than a drum. Mr. Lowry sat in his swivel chair, his back turned to the group, thinking. Suggestions for the way out came from all sides. Suddenly Mr. Lowry turned around, I can see the radiance of his face now, the twinkle in his eye. He drew on his fund of humorous stories. This had an electrifying effect. It put the group in a mood to carry on with their burden.

When it became clear that the company could not be saved, there was a scramble to extricate the stockholders from the wreckage. In return for an additional investment and a cancellation of their stock certificates, the eastern bankers finally agreed to release the Minneapolis men from further liability. Eustis quotes a letter written by Lowry on the stationery of the Holland House in New York:

> While Mr. Sterling has not absolutely promised, I am very well satisfied that as soon as you get the stock all corralled or deposited with Judge Koon, so that the decree can be entered, we can get the eastern stockholders to furnish money enough to take up all the western debts. This is very important and I want to have it done while I am here as there may be some hitch after I leave. To this end, won't you please get in all the stock outstanding at once? You will probably have to send someone out to Iowa, or as the stockholder there is a widow, you had better go yourself and then you surely will get the stock. Now my boy do your duty and we will soon have the

coast clear so the bankers can bother you about something else.

Among the "something elses" with which the bankers were undoubtedly concerned was the Twin City Rapid Transit Company.

Shortly before the real panic struck Wall Street, Lowry had raised an additional $2 million, or barely enough to cover the floating debt which had resulted from the final phase of the construction program. Again the funds came from a syndicate headed by Kuhn, Loeb and Company, and the terms were harsh. The loan was repayable in installments of $250,000 on the first days of 1895, 1896, and 1897, with the balance of $1,250,000 falling due on January 1, 1898. Furthermore, the loan was secured by all of the stock of the Minneapolis Street Railway Company and the St. Paul City Railway Company. In other words, if Lowry failed to come up with the funds to meet one of the January 1 installments, the entire system would become the property of the New York bankers. As the only source of cash to meet the installments, operating earnings had now become even more crucial. And earnings were not meeting earlier expectations. Along with the panic, there arrived on the scene a new and unlikely competitor. One of the company histories described it as follows:

> Coincidentally with the slump in business due to the financial panic, the company had to contend with severe bicycle competition during the years 1893, 1894, 1895, and 1896. Everybody remembers the extent to which the bicycle was used for business and recreation purposes during those years, by all classes of people, rich and poor, men and women, young and old. Between the hours of 7:30 and 9:00 A.M. each week day, all the principal streets leading to the downtown district were crowded with bicycles, and the same condition prevailed in the evening, which greatly reduced the company's revenues. This so-called Bicycle Craze hit the liveryman as hard as it hit the Minneapolis Street Railway. Outdoor recreation parties on holidays, Sundays and evenings always took to the bicycle. Bicycling was carried to such an extent that many fashionable

The bicycle craze during the middle 1890s proved difficult competition for the streetcar company.

people went to the theatre on their wheels instead of in carriages. It is hard to give the public an adequate idea of the extent to which the bicycle craze cut into the Street Railway earnings.

In 1892, net earnings after all charges had reached a new high of $241,000. They were expected to rise to $375,000 in 1893. But, as a result of the depression and the bicycle competition, the year 1893 produced a disappointing profit of $116,000, less than enough to meet an annual installment on the loan from Kuhn, Loeb and Company, to say nothing of the continuing capital needs, such as new track and new cars.

If the earnings were not increased, the company would face bankruptcy. Since there was no likelihood, under the terms of the franchises, of increasing the five-cent fare, an increase in earnings could only be accomplished by a decrease in expenses.

The job of reducing expenses is never easy and is usually painful, but in this case, it had to be done. The wage rates were cut by

10 percent, which was probably not unusual in that depression year. The mileage of the cars was decreased by 12½ percent with an equivalent reduction in service and a much higher volume of complaints. Finally, the number of employees in every department was reduced. As a result, operating costs in 1894 were reduced by $367,000, and profits rose from $116,000 to $221,000. In 1895, expenses were down another $103,000, and profits rose to $259,000. The patient was getting better.

On April 26, 1894, Lowry wrote to Higginson: "Since this panic commenced, both Mr. Goodrich and myself have been studying very hard as to how to operate the road economically and at the same time keep up the physical condition of the road; I think you will concede, after a full examination, that we have succeeded even beyond our own expectations."

At about the same time, there appeared another opportunity to cut expenses. Producing the electricity to move the cars was one of the chief expenses. As early as 1890, when Lowry was negotiating with Villard, the two men had proposed building a "lower dam" below St. Anthony Falls and using the cheap water power so produced to generate electricity for the streetcar system. For a number of reasons, including Villard's misfortunes, this plan was abandoned. But Lowry had not forgotten it. Toward the end of 1894, he sailed to London to talk with the men who controlled Pillsbury-Washburn Flour Mills Company. This corporation had been lately organized by London capitalists to acquire the Pillsbury and Washburn mills, and along with them, all of the water power rights at and below St. Anthony Falls.

The following letter from Lowry to Higginson was dated January 17, 1895:

> I wrote you the other day concerning the probability of lease by the Twin City Rapid Transit Co. of the water power to be created by the building of a dam below the Falls of St. Anthony. When in London I had a written proposition from the parties interested, that if the Street Railway Co. would pay

them an annual rental of $91,000, they would make the expenditure and build the dam. I enclose printed report of same, which has been verified by other engineers of undoubted ability and national reputation. This report is considered very conservative. The lease is now being prepared and I will bring it up at our next Directors' meeting at N.Y. My own judgment is that it will net a revenue to the Street Railway Co. of at least $150,000 per year and perhaps more. It is intended to operate all our electric cars both in St. Paul and Minneapolis by water power. We can supply various small industries with the surplus power and get a large income from that source.

The Pillsbury-Washburn Company put $953,000 into this project, and when it was completed in 1897, it was declared one of the greatest engineering feats of the century. It was also notable in the boost it gave to the earnings of the Twin City Rapid Transit Company.

With earnings on the upswing but still pressed for cash, Lowry decided to try a new form of financing. On December 22, 1894, he wrote to Higginson: "I explained to your Mr. Jackson the other day that we had decided to issue $3,000,000 of 7% Preferred Stock and offer from a million to a million and a half of it at the present time to the stockholders. I am very sure that it will be better for them all to take their share of this stock, but they can judge for themselves."

At the same time, Lowry produced a pamphlet which consisted largely of two reports of examination made by Frank Trumbull, a respected engineer from Denver. Dated January 18, 1893, and June 9, 1894, and addressed to Kuhn, Loeb and Company, who had instigated them, these reports were highly complimentary and doubtless played a large part in persuading the New York bankers to continue their financial support. The second report ended with the following words:

In conclusion, I will say that I have unabated confidence in the future of the Twin City Rapid Transit Company's properties. You have now paid for your experience as pioneer in electric railway operations on a large scale, and having acquired the experience in a hitherto untried field, you ought from now on to reap a sure reward. I think you may well have confidence in the future of St. Paul and Minneapolis and any increase in gross earnings ought to be largely *net*, if the present vigilant scrutiny of details is continued.

Very truly yours,
Frank Trumbull

As it turned out, the Boston stockholders would have been wise to take Lowry's advice and buy their share of the new preferred stock. But they didn't. Nobody had much free money in 1895, and, besides, the Bostonians' interest in their Twin Cities investment was obviously waning.

Finding little enthusiasm among his stockholders, Lowry made a second visit to London, where he presumably further exposed the virtues of his company to the men he had met while negotiating his lease of the water power rights.

On May 3, 1895, Lowry wrote a rather curt note to Higginson to advise him that $1,130,000 of the new preferred stock had been sold, "which is all we care to place for the present."

With the success of the preferred stock issue, the worst of Lowry's problems were behind him. But it would be hard to overstate the difficulties which he had overcome.

One of the stories surviving this dark period concerns Lowry and Francis A. Chamberlain, president of the Security National Bank. One morning Chamberlain, a frugal citizen, was standing on a corner of Hennepin Avenue, waiting for a streetcar to take him to his office in the Guaranty building, when Lowry, in a magnificent carriage, swept down Lowry Hill and drew up to offer the banker a ride downtown. As it happened, Lowry had recently prevailed on Chamberlain to increase the bank's loan on the grounds that, if the bank would not do so, the company would go under and the bank would have a sure loss on the loan which it had already made. So it

Lowry's magnificent carriage

was natural for Chamberlain to comment on the luxury of Lowry's brand new carriage and splendid horses complete with new gold harness. Lowry laughed and readily acknowledged that his new outfit had been purchased with the bank's funds. He then accompanied Chamberlain to his office and is said to have convinced him that Lowry's life-style was as essential to the streetcar company's credit rating as its balance sheet was.

At the time of Lowry's death, Chamberlain was quoted by the *Journal*: "Mr. Lowry was, undoubtedly, one of the most beloved men in Minneapolis, by all classes of people. He was one of the bravest men I ever saw. I have seen Mr. Lowry when things were going hard with him and I have seen him when everything was bright and cheerful, and he was always the same. Apparently he never lost his nerve. In the very hardest times he was the most alert and resourceful and was equal to all occasions."

J. F. Calderwood, the streetcar company's auditor during those years, used to relate this episode, which was printed in the *St. Paul Dispatch* of February 6, 1909:

> In 1893, the year of the panic, Tom and I were tramping up
> and down Wall Street trying to get a loan for the Transit

Company. It was either a loan or bankruptcy and no small loan either. Our security was first-class, but what's security in a time of panic?

Well, at last we found a banker who seemed to have kept his head. He answered that, secured by such property as ours, he and his associates, if they advanced a half million or so, would be sure to get their money back with interest sooner or later, they couldn't lose, he thought. We thought so too and the matter was all arranged then and there, except the final formalities. Those could be attended to next day. Down in the Street, you know, it's a mighty big loan that can't be made within 48 hours, if its going to be made at all.

But when we came back next morning, perfectly confident that our troubles were over, Mr. Banker spoke up glumly and briefly.

"Sorry, gentlemen; it's all off. My friends can't see it just as I do," and once more we started on our peddling tour of the financial district, not knowing where we could raise $10,000.

"We didn't accomplish much," was all Tom said.

Just then when I was too gloomy and self-absorbed to notice an elephant, Tom caught sight of a little red-haired "newsy" with a specially bright smile and persistent manner. Tom bought the boy's entire stock in trade, and then asked him what he was going to do with the money. The kid said his mother was a janitress and lived in the basement of a house on Sixth Avenue and Fifty-Ninth Street, "and didn't have much fun" and he was going to get her a dandy Thanksgiving dinner.

First Tom rather doubted the newsy. But when the boy offered "to go and prove it," Tom called a cab, bundled me and the boy into it, and drove off with us up to the basement home on Sixth Avenue. The story, we found, was true enough. Tom chatted a bit with the janitress and then walked with me around the corner to a grocery store. He bought a big basket of provisions, toted it back to the basement, handed it over to the mother as a little present from her boy's "uncle" and hurried back laughing to our cab. As we drove down to the Holland House, Tom remarked: "Well, I guess we did accomplish something today, after all."

It was only a coincidence, of course, but we got all the money we needed the next morning.

There are many other funny stories and a few sad ones that are still told about Lowry's battle for survival. His sense of humor, his optimism, and his humanity apparently carried him through a period of crisis which would have proved too rough for most men. But the storm got almost too severe for even a man of Lowry's buoyancy.

In those days the rules of the investment game were more hazardous than they are today. The stocks of banks and most other financial institutions were subject to so-called "double liability." If the company failed, the stockholder not only lost his original investment, but could also be called on to forfeit an equal amount of cash if needed to pay off the creditors. Lowry's investment in the Northwestern Guaranty Loan Company, now hopelessly bankrupt, carried this "double liability."

Another financial hazard of the time was the custom of requiring a company's prinicipal stockholders to personally guaranty a company's indebtedness. For example, the bank notes of the Northwestern Knitting Company, which was finding the going very rough, were personally guarantied by Lowry along with Clinton Morrison and Charles Pillsbury. And most of the bonds of the streetcar companies, about $6 million, were personally guarantied by Lowry. If the streetcar companies had gone over the approaching brink of bankruptcy, Lowry's entire fortune would have gone over with them. Lowry's real estate was also in the doldrums, and his countless friends were more of a liability than an asset. Many of them were closer to the brink than he was, and in a number of instances, Lowry loaned them or gave them thousands of dollars which he could ill afford.

One such friend was Colonel John T. West, the proprietor of the hotel which Lowry had done so much to promote. Burdened by its $400,000 mortgage, the West Hotel had been a losing venture, especially after the panic had set in. Colonel West was heavily in debt, hard pressed by creditors, and in failing spirits. Tom Lowry, thinking back to the grand opening of 1884 and the testimonial dinner given for him in 1892, decided it was time for another bash, this one as a testimonial to all that John West had done for Minneapolis. The first two events had each been attended by about 350 men. In the depression year of 1896, Lowry turned out more than 400 men for a banquet in honor of John West and presided over one of the city's most heart-warming occasions.

There is no record of the number of banks in New York and Minneapolis which were carrying and worrying about Lowry's indebtedness. But his $50,000 debt to the Northwestern National Bank of Minneapolis must have been the most personal and the most embarrassing. His father-in-law, Dr. Goodrich, had been an original stockholder and director of the Northwestern Bank, and since 1883, Lowry had served as a member of the bank's board together with such friends as Martin Koon, Charles A. Pillsbury, T. B. Janney, and W. H. Dunwoody. At the depth of the depression in January 1896, with his indebtedness under criticism, Lowry resigned his chair on the board.

A further insight into this period of Lowry's life is offered by the following excerpt from the obituary which appeared in the *New York Times* at the time of his death (February 5, 1909):

> Mr. Lowry's business and financial career had not been one of unbroken sunshine. During the reorganization of the street railway and in the panicky years which followed, some of his projects were dangerously near their end. He sold or mortgaged private interests and even moved his family into cheaper quarters and rented his palatial home to those who could afford to live in luxury. In this way he was able to stem the tide and to prove to those who doubted his prophecy that great things were in store for the enterprises in which he was interested.

The long road finally had its turning, and as the "great things" began to materialize, the street railway company led the way.

The Trolley Catches On

While a large part of the country's new system of electric street railways was actually built in the early 1890s, it was not until 1898 or 1899 that the trolley really arrived as a thrilling new chapter in the American Dream. Held back by superstition, financial depression, and the bicycle craze, people flirted cautiously with this new invention during its first years. But then, in a sudden burst of enthusiasm, they embraced it as a way of life. Amusement parks sprang up in the outskirts of the cities, and the streetcars which had been carrying growing numbers of people to work were now jammed by crowds bent on weekend excursions. All of a sudden, the trolley was fashionable.

Roy L. McCardell's poem, featured in *Trolley Car Treasury* by Frank Rowsome, catches the spirit of the day:

THE SONG OF THE TROLLEY

I am coming. I am coming. Hark you hear my motor
 humming.
For the trolley's come to conquer, so you cannot keep it back.
And Zip! the sparks are flashing, as the car goes onward
 dashing
While the wheels are whirring smoothly along a perfect track.

'Tis vain then to delay me, for you cannot stop or stay me.
Though old fogies fought against me for I went too fast, they
 said.

And they talked of death and danger to the native and the
  stranger—
Oh! a frightful state they were in from my wire overhead.

.   .   .   .

Hear me whizzing through the highways—see me brightening
  up the byways,
Annihilating distance as I merry speed along:
I bring new life and faces to old sleeping towns and places
And a million homes are brighter for the music of my song.

.   .   .   .

I've no palace car or sleeper, but I carry people cheaper,
And I bring the breath of country to the toilers of the town;
I increase the mail facilities—freight carrying abilities
Are among my many virtues and I cannot be kept down.

.   .   .   .

Yes, I'm coming, I am coming, don't you hear my motor
  humming?
For the trolley's here to conquer and you cannot keep it back;
And 'Zip'! the sparks are flashing as the car goes onward
  dashing
Yes the trolley's come and conquered, so look out! and clear
  the track!

The published results of the Twin City Rapid Transit Company, organized by Lowry in 1891 to combine the streetcar systems
of Minneapolis and St. Paul, chart a trend which was probably
similar in most American cities. (See table on facing page.)

At the low point of the depression in 1895, the Twin Cities
streetcars were carrying about 110,000 passengers a day. In 1899
there were 140,000 riders, and by 1901, the number had reached
175,000. On August 15, 1899, after 24 years in the streetcar business, Tom Lowry was at last able to announce a dividend on the

RESULTS OF THE TWIN CITY RAPID TRANSIT COMPANY
(thousands of dollars)

	Gross Revenue	Operating Expense	Operating Income	Interest & Dividends on Preferred Stock	Surplus	Dividends on Common Stock
1892	2,187	1,449	738	498	240	0
1893	2,188	1,450	738	622	116	0
1894	2,008	1,083	920	700	220	0
1895	1,989	980	1,009	750	259	0
1896	2,059	995	1,064	764	300	0
1897	2,009	1,002	1,007	771	235	0
1898	2,170	1,019	1,151	778	373	0
1899	2,523	1,157	1,366	815	551	375
1900	2,839	1,305	1,534	829	705	450
1901	3,174	1,415	1,759	877	882	600

common stock And the common stock, which had been selling for $10 or less when it could be sold at all, was finally worth something. Now listed on the New York Stock Exchange, the stock sold for as much as $88 in 1899, $109 in 1901, and $129 in 1902. Not only had the electric streetcar become a fashionable conveyance, but the stocks and bonds of streetcar companies had also become fashionable investments. During most of his life, Lowry had been fairly alone in his faith in the streetcar business. Suddenly he was amid a crowd of eager investors. He must have enjoyed it!

As the earnings grew and the surplus cash flowed into the bank, there were plenty of opportunities to spend it. One of the first was a project to build, rather than buy, the streetcars which were the backbone of the business.

A shop was completed in 1898 on the company's property at Thirty-First Street and Nicollet Avenue. Its first product was a private car for Tom Lowry. With mahogany paneling, draped curtains, upholstered sofa, and wicker armchairs, this was a truly lux-

Tom Lowry's luxurious private car carried many notable visitors on tours of the Twin Cities.

urious vehicle, and it carried many notable visitors, including Teddy Roosevelt and William McKinley, on sightseeing tours of the Twin Cities. The private car was followed by 22 streetcars completed in 1898, 31 in 1899, and a growing number in succeeding years. In 1907 the Thirty-First Street shop was superseded by a larger facility, more centrally located at Snelling and University in the Midway district of the Twin Cities. With 500 employees, the Snelling shop became one of the area's principal manufacturers. And it was producing a streetcar second to none in quality and comfort.

In 1898 the remaining cable line was replaced by an electric line with a counterweight system to haul the cars up the steep bluff at Selby Avenue. The Cable Lines, which had been expensive to build, had proven even more expensive to operate. Each line required its own powerhouse to drive the long heavy cables, which produced a steady flow of accidents and breakdowns. As the last cable car was retired, Lowry must have blessed the day he had chosen to scrap the Minneapolis cable equipment in favor of the newfangled electric power.

As more and more people grew interested in the amusement parks in the outskirts of the cities, Lowry found a way to serve them. The St. Paul and White Bear Railroad, organized in 1889 and electrified in 1892, was running cars over 11 miles of track from St. Paul east to White Bear Lake, where a rather primitive amusement park had been developed. Victims of the depression, this streetcar line and the Wildwood Amusement Park were acquired by Lowry's company in 1898. As the line was improved and the amusement park expanded, Sunday at Wildwood Amusement Park became increasingly popular. A dance hall featured quality orchestras and exhibition dances. Fresh lake fish dinners were served in the main pavillion. And entertainment included the Fun Factory (with distorting mirrors), a photo gallery, a shooting gallery, a penny arcade, and a carousel. For the brave, there was a roller coaster.

To balance the excursions east of St. Paul, a similar location west of Minneapolis was sought, and Lake Minnetonka was a natural. Twenty miles long and four miles wide, the lake consists of more than 20 bays, with a shoreline of 300 miles, all beautifully wooded. The old Motor Line had run steam-driven trains from Lake Harriet to Excelsior during the years 1882–86, and the Twin

This shot of an Excelsior doubledecker was taken in 1903.

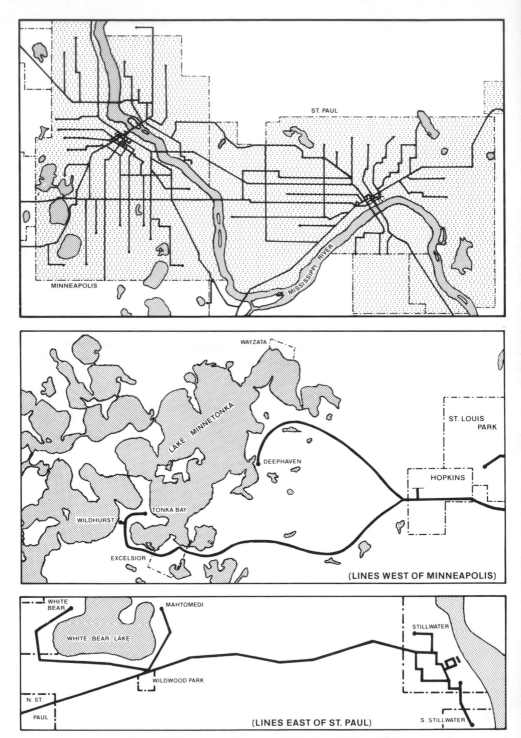

Transit Lines in and around the Twin Cities, 1916

The Twin City Rapid Transit Company developed an amusement park at Big Island, two miles from the Excelsior docks on Lake Minnetonka.

City Rapid Transit Company had inherited much of this right-of-way. In 1905 construction of a 14-mile track from Lake Harriet to Excelsior got under way; it was completed in June 1906. Subsequent lines extended service to Deephaven and Tonka Bay, where the company acquired the 200-room Tonka Bay Hotel.

The company also purchased 65 acres on Big Island, two miles from the Excelsior docks, and developed it into a park with the conventional amusement features of the day, together with picnic facilities and superior band concerts in the Music Casino. John Philip Sousa's band was among the well-known performers. The park's architecture was Spanish and featured a 200-foot water tower modeled on a structure in Seville. At night, Big Island Park and the ferryboats linking it to Excelsior produced a blaze of music, light, and excitement.

While a large number and variety of excursion boats had been operating on Lake Minnetonka since the 1860s, there were no reg-

ularly scheduled routes. In the winter of 1905–6 the shops undertook to build six fast, safe steamboats which resembled streetcars
down to their yellow paint, and which would extend scheduled, de-
pendable transportation to the extensive shoreline of Lake Minnetonka. Boasting a speed of 15 miles an hour, the boats were 70 feet
long and 14 feet wide, and they carried 200 passengers. Four regular routes were established, all originating at the Excelsior dock
with hourly service on weekdays and half-hour service on Sundays.
One of the routes was described as follows:

EXCELSIOR–MINNETONKA BEACH LINE

DOCKS	MILES
Excelsior	0.00
Tonka Bay	1.10
Wheelers (Big Island)	1.85
Arcola	2.72
Minnetonka Beach	3.22

Running time was 18 minutes outbound and 22 minutes in-
bound. The minimum fare between any two points was 10 cents; a
round-trip ride cost 20 cents. Transportation by ferryboat from Excelsior to Big Island Park was included in a 50-cent round-trip
ticket from Minneapolis. So a Sunday at Lake Minnetonka was a
moderately priced popular adventure.

As the system expanded, the demand for electricity grew. While
the water power plant at the lower falls had performed admirably,
it was no longer adequate, especially in times of low water in the
river. In 1903 a new generating plant was built just up the river,
and it was steam powered and designed to supplement the output
of the water power plant regardless of the water level. Five years
later, another water power station was built on Hennepin Island.

At the time of Tom Lowry's death in 1909, the Twin City Rapid Transit Company was an impressive enterprise and a model of
urban transportation. The system stretched 48 miles from Still-
water to Excelsior, with 368 miles of track in service. The clean,

speedy streetcars were 50 feet long and seated 50 passengers each, while the early horsecars were one-fifth the size and seated one-fifth as many people. The company was fully integrated even to the production of its own electricity and streetcars. It was the largest employer in the area and the most important force in shaping the growth of the Twin Cities. Its common stock, paying a regular 6 percent dividend, was regarded as an investment suitable for widows and orphans. The trolley had indeed arrived, especially in Minneapolis and St. Paul.

As the streetcar business began to prosper and the financial crisis receded, the Lowrys could devote more time to the community's social life. As in most other cities, the social functions of those days were taken seriously and were highly formalized.

As early as 1889, the *Blue Book* listed the names of 15,000 of "the most prominent people in the Twin Cities" together with lists of the members of the principal clubs, and a section was devoted to "hints on etiquette." From the latter feature, a matron could learn the fine points of acceptable decorum in the parlor and the dining room, the procedures to be followed in introductions, and the rules of the fine art of "calling." Most of the ladies had a fixed day of the week when they could be found "at home" and when their acquaintances made their appearance at least once a year between the hours of 1:00 and 6:00 P.M. to pay a visit and leave their calling cards with the proper corner turned down to indicate the nature of the call. The *Blue Book* gave an admonition which might be as helpful today as it was in 1889: "When making calls avoid anything either in conversation or action calculated to excite unfavorable remarks. Boisterousness is especially to be avoided; so are over loud talk, whispering, criticisms on religious subjects and political disputations. It is exceedingly illbred to repeat scandal or to discuss people or topics of questionable character."

When in public one is warned: "As much care should be taken to exhibit good breeding in public places as in drawing rooms or at formal receptions. A true lady or gentleman never forgets the conventionalities of life under any circumstances. Always be considerate of the rights and feelings of others. While it is barely permissible for a gentleman to smoke in the streets, it would be exceedingly rude to smoke in the company of ladies."

Although Beatrice Lowry had been regarded as a social leader ever since her marriage, one doubts that the customs in the mansion on Lowry Hill could have been quite as formal as those listed in the *Blue Book*. Tom Lowry's disposition, so often described as hilarious, was hardly compatible with Victorian solemnities. But this didn't preclude the Lowrys' taking a very active role in the social affairs of the community. In fact, Beatrice took the leading part in launching the most important social function of the day.

On August 24, 1898, the first meeting of an organization to be known as "The Hostesses" was recorded as follows:

> An informal meeting was called at Mrs. Lowry's August 24 to consider arrangements for a Ball or Series of Balls to be given this winter with a view to making them a permanent event each winter.
>
> A temporary organization was effected, Mrs. Lowry Chairman and Mrs. Martin Secretary. Mrs. Lowry read letters outlining the manner in which a similar series is conducted in New York.
>
> Informal discussion followed upon the place of entertaining, the number of entertainments, the name of the organization etc. etc. Mrs. Lowry and Mrs. Carpenter were asked to see Mr. West in regard to putting down a hard wood floor in the dining room of the West Hotel with a view to holding parties there.
>
> By request of Mrs. Tenney, Mrs. Lowry named Mrs. Harrison, Mrs. Carpenter and Mrs. Winter as a committee on organization and nomination.
>
> One Ball only was decided on the first winter to occur Friday evening November 18th. It was decided that nothing was to be given to the papers for publication until all the arrangements were complete.
>
> Ella S. Martin, Secretary

Beatrice Lowry founded the Hostesses, a group that organized major social events.

At subsequent meetings, rules were adopted and a list of 50 hostesses was drawn up. Each was allotted 10 tickets; this brought the number of invitations to 500.

The *Tribune's* story on the first ball included a statement of purpose:

> The Hostesses' organization is the demonstration of a clearly defined social theory, held by a prominent number of women of the city, that there should be a common meeting ground for the many circles which must necessarily be small and personal, where young and old, grave and gay, pioneers and newcomers, may be brought together to find out what is best in each, and through this more appreciative knowledge of each other to be broadened and ennobled by better and truer views of the life around them. The inclusive idea is not being confined to philanthropies and education, and the Hostesses have scored a great triumph in the application of the idea to Minneapolis Society.

The article went on to describe the elaborate decorations, including oriental carpets, large palms in bronze jardinieres, and a profusion of ferns and chrysanthemums. One of the unstated purposes of the Hostesses was the introduction of debutantes, and at the first ball, these were Misses Nellie Winston, Eugenia Wilson, and Marion Towne, whose low-cut silk and velvet garments were fully described.

The first ball was a great success and became, as an annual occurrence, the highlight of the Minneapolis social calendar. For 10 years, Beatrice Lowry presided as chairman of the management committee and was generally regarded the leader of Minneapolis "society."

Last Days

"TOM LOWRY IS DEAD!"

With incredible swiftness the news spread among the employees of the Twin City Rapid Transit Company. It went from mouth to mouth in a hushed, awed whisper: "Our old man is dead."

It was not the fact that Mr. Thomas Lowry, the President of the Twin City Rapid Transit Co. and of the Soo Line was dead, but that Tom Lowry, the friend and counselor of his employees, who was affectionately and familiarly known as "the old man," had died—that was different.

Those who saw the effect of the announcement on the men who handle the brass cranks and collect the coin could have little doubt but that their grief was deep and sincere.

These words came from the *Minneapolis Tribune* of February 5, 1909, and they came as no surprise. For five years Lowry had been fighting a recurrence of the tuberculosis which had first brought him to Minneapolis and which he had overcome as a young man. He had been relatively inactive since the turn of the century, and, since 1905, he had been a sick man. Fortunately, his competent brother-in-law, Calvin Goodrich, was qualified to manage a streetcar system which was now an established success. And Lowry's son, Horace, elected a director of the company in 1903, was getting settled in the business. At the time of his father's death, Horace, who had spent two years as an electrician in the Snelling shops, was superintendent of the Minneapolis division.

While Lowry's death had been no surprise, the public's reaction to it was. On February 6, the day of the funeral, Mayor Haynes, for the first time in the city's history, ordered the flags on all public and private buildings flown at half-mast. For five minutes during the funeral, every streetcar stood still. And the newspapers were flooded with phone calls suggesting ways in which Tom Lowry could be memorialized.

This reaction to the death of a capitalist brought the following comment from the *New York Evening Post* (February 13, 1909):

> The genuine grief manifested in St. Paul and Minneapolis over the death of Thomas Lowry, President of the Twin City Rapid Transit Company, conveys a plain lesson. When his fellow-townsmen acclaim a man as a public spirited citizen and, when that person happens to be the owner of the greatest public service corporation in the community, the verdict has unusual interest. In a day when mere connection with a public utilities company is so often viewed as an a priori ground for suspicion, and when the management of street railways, in particular, has been the object of so much attack, the position that Mr. Lowry held was unique. It was through him that St. Paul and Minneapolis were welded together by a railroad system which its patrons did not look upon with angry derision, but were wont to boast of as the best in the country. Mr. Lowry appears to have been a captain of industry who at the same time was so fortunate as to absorb some ideas of social service and social responsibility. He was not without his critics, but to read of the esteem in which he was held by a great variety and number of men, from Gov. Johnson to Cyrus Northrop, makes a citizen of New York or Philadelphia look about and wonder why they have not his fellow.

The last years of Tom Lowry's life were relatively uneventful and almost placid. He spent winters in the warm, dry air of Phoenix and San Antonio. And his last four summers found him settled into a newly built house on his farm, which lay on the banks of the Mississippi near Monticello, some 35 miles northwest of Minneapolis.

Lowry's farm home lay on the banks of the Mississippi near Monticello, Minnesota.

Alice Smith of Brown's Valley, Minnesota, was nine years old in the summer of 1905; her father, a surveyor, was helping with the landscaping of the new house. Mrs. Smith remembered Lowry as a quiet, modest, and friendly man who conversed with a nine-year-old girl in the same tone and manner he used with adults. She recalled that his property contained three ponds fed by a meandering stream, and when someone suggested that the stream be straightened, Lowry replied: "Oh, no, let it keep on wandering around. It's got lots of time."

During these leisurely days, Lowry renewed some of his earlier interests. The Lincoln funeral car, which was displayed at the St. Louis World's Fair of 1904, had carried the body of Lowry's hero on a ceremonial tour from Washington to its resting place in Springfield. Learning of its availability, Lowry bought the car in 1905 and brought it to Minneapolis, where it was placed on dis-

The Abraham Lincoln funeral car as it appeared in 1908 at the 42nd Encampment of the Grand Army of the Republic in Minneapolis.

play at a respectful but convenient distance from the sales office which was finding Columbia Heights lots so hard to sell. And it served as a focal point for the 42nd Encampment of the Grand Army of the Republic convened at Minneapolis in 1908. The car stood in Columbia Heights for six years until it was destroyed by a grass fire.

It was at this time that Lowry began to write his *Reminiscences of Abraham Lincoln*, which, published after his death, is a pleasant, informal description of Lincoln as young Tom Lowry knew him in Illinois.

As the streetcar company continued to prosper and as the general economy recovered from the panic, Lowry's personal finances became more orderly. On January 2, 1894, he assigned virtually all of his personal assets to the Central Trust Company of New York in what appeared to be a consolidation of his many obligations. In April 1902, following the sharp increase in the market value of Twin City Rapid Transit Company stock, the Central Trust Company returned to him the assets which had not been needed to satisfy his debts, and while his fortune had been sadly depleted, he was no longer virtually bankrupt. The first evidence of his relative prosperity was the revival of his philanthropies.

The Methodists of Pleasant View, his home town in Illinois, had been struggling for several years to find the money to build a new church. Finally, toward the end of 1906, one of the Malcolmsons, who had bought the old Lowry farm, thought to write Tom Lowry about their problem. By return mail, Lowry responded with a check for $5,000, and the church was built the next year.

Another and probably deeper interest was Lombard College in Galesburg. Along with his pastor, Marion Shutter, Lowry had for some years been an active and much interested trustee of Lombard. When the college undertook a drive to establish a $100,000 endowment fund, Lowry was among the first to respond. He is also credited with providing the impetus which put the drive over the top.

The *Lombard College Annual* of 1907 says:

> In November, Mr. Lowry of Minneapolis, who had pledged $10,000, being of failing health, remarked that he thought there should be some time limit to the pledges and accordingly announced that his pledge would hold good until December 31, 1906. Hence, in order to save this large pledge it was necessary to complete the fund before the old year died. This action on the part of Mr. Lowry was a wise one. Friends saw the necessity for immediate action and brought considerations and delays to an end. By the date determined upon, the last pledge was in and the task was done.

While these contributions in Illinois were probably unknown in Minnesota, Lowry's efforts on behalf of the Parade Stadium were close to home. Of the 12 blocks comprising this new park, Lowry donated 5; he also contributed the money required for landscaping. The property was originally a part of the Goodrich farm.

When Lowry died, he was worth somewhat less than a million dollars. Among his assets were 3,000 shares of common stock of the Twin City Rapid Transit Company, or just 2 percent of the stock outstanding.

The funeral took place in the home on Lowry Hill and was followed the next day by a memorial service in the Church of the Redeemer. At the latter service, Dr. Marion Shutter spoke of Lowry's long and close association with the church. His words were recorded in the *Minneapolis Journal* of February 8, 1909:

> When I was gathering my material for the life of my predecessor, Dr. Tuttle, I went to Mr. Lowry for his recollections. It was about a year after Dr. Tuttle began preaching that Mr. Lowry came to Minneapolis. To use his own expression, his baggage at that time was quite condensed. He was met by a bustling citizen who was a devoted admirer of the Universalist preacher and urged the young man to be sure to hear him the very next Sunday. Without any strong religious preferences save that he had been educated at a Universalist College, the young man decided to follow this advice. So the next Sunday, he proceeded by a cow path, across open fields to the frame church at the corner of Fourth Avenue South and Fifth Street.
>
> The preacher interested him from the start. "Never," he said long afterward, "had I heard a minister who so impressed me. I felt that is the man for me." He became a regular attendant, and a strong friendship grew up between him and Dr. Tuttle. He was often at the pastor's home and with many other young men who visited the home on Chicago Avenue, he became as one of the family. The friendship ripened into affection and 32 years after the young stranger from the country had found his way to the church, the old pastor, broken in health and but a few paces from the journey's end, wrote to the famous man of affairs:
>
> My dear Mr. Lowry:
>
> You will never fade from my mind as long as I have any mind. You are a successful man, not alone because of the thousands you have amassed, but because you have kept intact the amiable spirit your creator gave you and won the good will and good wishes of your neighbors and of all who ever knew you.
>
> That is just what everyone is saying about Mr. Lowry today.

While Lowry seldom spoke in terms of religion, the Church of the Redeemer was undoubtedly a strong influence in his life. As a friend, a trustee, and a contributor, he supported Shutter as strongly as he had supported Tuttle. And his religious convictions were probably of considerable importance during his darker days.

Soon after Tom Lowry's funeral, the demand for a memorial materialized. The Thomas Lowry Memorial Association was formed with Martin B. Koon as its president, and it raised, among Lowry's friends, the funds for a splendid bronze statue. Executed by Karl Bitter, a brilliant New York sculptor, the lifesize statue was placed on Lowry Hill at the intersection of Hennepin and Lyndale Avenues, and it was dedicated on August 18, 1915. On one side of the supporting masonry was written, "Be this community strong and enduring, it will do homage to the men who guided its growth," and on the other side, "The lesson of a public-spirited life is as a tree ever bearing new fruit."

The *Minneapolis Journal* of August 18, 1915, reported that at the dedication service, Dr. Shutter said: "It was fitting that Karl Bitter should make the statue of Thomas Lowry. And how grandly he has done his work! This heroic figure needs no emblazoned name to identify its original. It seems almost as if Karl Bitter had stood by the door of that mausoleum in Lakewood Cemetery and had said: 'Tom Lowry, come forth!' for this is a veritable resurrection."

In the late 1960s, when Interstate 94 was tunneled through Lowry Hill, the statue was moved to a small park at Hennepin and Twenty-Fourth Street. By this time, the old Lowry home had been replaced by the North American Life building, the Walker Art Center, and the Guthrie Theater. Gone too were the West Hotel, the Guaranty Loan building, the first public library, and most of the other landmarks of the Minneapolis that Tom Lowry and his contemporaries knew.

But the spirit and the personality of the place seem curiously unchanged. The city has always been known for its gumption, its optimism, its generosity, and its concern for the underdog. These are the qualities which Tom Lowry admired and helped to develop. He would immensely enjoy finding them alive and well today in his beloved Minneapolis.

Subsequent History of the Twin City Rapid Transit Co.

After Tom Lowry's death in 1909, the Twin City Rapid Transit Company continued to expand its facilities and its patronage. While automobiles were becoming more common, they were still regarded as a rich man's toy rather than a means of transportation. But following World War I, when Henry Ford and others began to mass-produce a car priced within the reach of the average family, the streetcar business went into a long, slow, steady decline.

In the peak year of 1922, the Twin City Lines carried 226 million passengers. They had carried 140 million at the time of Lowry's death. By 1940 the volume was down to 104 million; it rebounded to 200 million during World War II; and then, as the automobiles started pouring off the assembly lines, the streetcar traffic began another slide with only 150 million riders by 1949.

During this 40-year period, the company was run by four presidents whose viewpoints and policies were much like Tom Lowry's. Calvin G. Goodrich, Lowry's brother-in-law, served until his death in 1915. He was followed by Lowry's son, Horace, who, upon his death in 1931, was succeeded by his right-hand man T. Julian McGill. D. J. Strouse, who worked his way up from accountant under Tom Lowry, presided during the difficult period 1936-1949.

As the traffic declined, the company made many operating adjustments, but the basic policies were much the same. The track and the cars were kept in first-class condition; the quality of service remained high; and the dividends continued to be few and far between. Following the relative prosperity of the World War II years, Strouse undertook a modernization of the equipment, including the purchase of 140 new streamlined streetcars.

This move, while popular with the riding public, was disappointing to the 2,000 stockholders who wanted some of the profits diverted to dividends rather than improvements. At this point, Charles Green, a New York financier, appealed to the stockholders to oust the Strouse management. In November 1949, Green was elected president of the company, and Minneapolis lawyer Fred Ossanna was appointed counsel.

As a result of numerous disagreements with Ossanna, Green sold his stock, resigned as president, and was succeeded by Ossanna in 1951. Ossanna plunged the Twin City Lines into a complete conversion from streetcars to buses. General Motors agreed to finance the purchase of 525 large motor buses and the conversion was completed in two years' time. The last of 700 streetcars was pulled off the track on June 19, 1954, and 400 miles of rail were sold for scrap.

Upon the discovery of irregularities in the disposition of some of the company's assets, Ossanna was convicted of fraud and was sent to prison. The management was assumed by a new group headed by Daniel Feidt, who in 1970 negotiated the sale of the system to the Metropolitan Transit Commission. The Twin City Rapid Transit Company, as a private enterprise, had come to the end of the line.

Appendix 1
Transportation Museums and Attractions

Travel Town
Department of Recreation and
    Parks
Griffith Park
Los Angeles, CA 90027
(213) 662-5874

California Railway Museum
State Highway 12
Rio Vista Junction, CA
mailing address:
c/o Secretary
1802 East Twenty-Third Street
Oakland, CA 94606
(415) 534-0071

Orange Empire Railway Museum
P.O. Box 548
Perris, CA 92370
(714) 657-2605

Colorado Railroad Museum
P.O. Box 10
Golden, Colorado 80401
(303) 279-4591

Branford Trolley Museum
Branford Electric Railway,
    East Haven
17 River Street
East Haven, CT 06512
(203) 467-6927

Warehouse Point Trolley
    Museum
58 North Road
P.O. Box 436
Warehouse Point, CT 06088
(203) 623-7417

The Fox River Line
RELIC Trolley Museum
P.O. Box 315
South Elgin, IL 60177
(312) 697-4676

Illinois Railway Museum
P.O. Box 431
Union, IL 60180
(815) 923-2488
(312) 262-2266 (for information)

Indiana Museum of Transport &
    Communication
P.O. Box 83
Noblesville, IN 46060
(317) 773-0300

Midwest Old Settlers and
    Threshers Association
Midwest Central Railroad
Route 1
Mt. Pleasant, IA 52641
(319) 385-8937 (Association)
(319) 385-2912 (Railroad)

Seashore Trolley Museum
Log Cabin Road
P.O. Box 220
Kennebunkport, ME 04046
(207) 967-2712

Baltimore Streetcar Museum
Baltimore Streetcar Museum, Inc.
P.O. Box 7184
Baltimore, MD 21218
(301) 547-0264

159

National Capital Trolley Museum
P.O. Box 5795
Bethesda, MD 20014
(301) 384-9797

Minnesota Transportation
    Museum, Minneapolis
P.O. Box 1300
Hopkins, MN 55343
(612) 729-2428

National Museum of Transport
3015 Barrett Station Road
St. Louis, MO 63122
(314) 965-6885

Trolleyville, U.S.A.
7100 B Columbia Road
Olmsted Falls, OH 44138
(216) 235-4725

Ohio Railway Museum
P.O. Box 171
Worthington, OH 43085
(614) 885-7345

Trolley Park
Star Route
Box 1318
Glenwood, OR 97120
(503) 357-3574

Railways to Yesterday, Orbisonia
328 North Twenty-Eighth Street
Allentown, PA 18104
(814) 447-9576 (*weekends only*)

Buckingham Valley Trolley
    Association, Buckingham
    Valley
3001 Robin Lane
Havertown, PA 19083

no phone; for possible help, call:
New Hope & Ivyland Railroad
(215) 862-5206

Arden Trolley Museum
2 miles north of Washington, PA,
    on North Main Street
organizational mail:
Pennsylvania Railway Museum
    Association
P.O. Box 832
Pittsburgh, PA 15230
(412) 225-5780 (*24 hours*)

Puget Sound and Snoqualmie
    Valley Railroad, Snoqualmie
Puget Sound Railway Historical
    Association
Box 3801
Seattle, WA 98124
(206) 888-0373

Yakima Interurban Trolley Lines
P.O. Box 124
Yakima, WA 98907
(509) 575-1700

Halston County Radial Railway,
    Rockwood
Ontario Electric Railway
    Historical Association
Box 121, Station "A"
Scarborough, Ontario
Canada M1K 5B9

Canadian Railway Museum
P.O. Box 148
St. Constant, Quebec
Canada J0L 1X0
(514) 632-2410

Appendix 2
Trolleys in the United States

The story of the Twin City Rapid Transit Company is a product of both the geography of Minneapolis-St. Paul and the personality of Tom Lowry, the man behind the system. Like that system, other companies in cities across the United States also reflected the needs of their regions and the characters of the people who shaped them.

Any account of United States trolleys should begin in Richmond, Virginia, where Frank J. Sprague was contracted in May 1887 to provide a complete electrical street railway system. A brilliant inventor who had worked for Thomas Edison, Sprague undertook the Richmond venture at the young age of 29. Unlike previous experimenters, he brought a formidable scientific background to bear upon the traction field.

Sprague's Richmond contract called for his firm to equip a 375-horsepower central-station power plant, to build an overhead power system on 12 miles of track (not yet built), and to provide motors for 40 cars, 30 of which would be operated at one time: an agreement that, given the realities of traction in 1887, "a prudent businessman would not ordinarily assume," as Sprague commented later. He encountered problems at every turn, including a case of typhoid fever for himself, an "execrable" track laid by an independent contractor, and 39 trolley-pole designs that were not feasible. Although difficulties continued, the line was opened for regular service in February 1888. On the first day, cars kept stopping suddenly because of a lack of proper oiling; soon afterward, bad weather gave the trolley wire a coat of ice. And motors kept causing problems: parts frequently burned out and needed rewiring; many had to be shipped to New York City to be rebuilt.

Yet the system did improve. The number of available cars increased gradually from 10 to 20 to 30 to 40 (operating at one time).

Trolleys at Delaware Avenue and B Street N.E. in Washington, D. C.

Once its mechanical problems were solved, Sprague's system eventually gained a nationwide reputation.

The Richmond system became a model for other cities to follow, and one of the first to do so was Boston, Massachusetts. By 1887, Henry M. Whitney had consolidated his railway system with three other local ones, and his West End Street Railway Company of Boston, the world's largest street railway system at the time, boasted 8,000 horses. Though he was thinking of adopting the cable system, Whitney took his general manager, Daniel F. Longstreet, to Richmond to view Sprague's electric system. Longstreet doubted the Richmond system's ability to avoid snarls of large groups of cars that became bunched together on short stretches of track.

Sprague put on a special "show" to convince the Boston businessmen of the electric system's worth. Late one night, after the Richmond cars had completed their regular routes, Sprague arranged for 22 of them to line up on a section of railway that was meant for the operation of only four cars at once. He gave a signal, and the cars' motormen started up, each pulling away when it was possible. Though the electrical drain was great—the lamps in the cars dimmed down considerably—every car eventually moved along. Whitney returned to Boston with great praise for electric systems and got permission from the city's board of aldermen to electrify his own. He used motors built by Sprague's company on all of his cars.

Other cities followed the leads of Richmond and Boston. Within two years, more than 200 electric street railway systems had sprung up in the United States, and more than half were equipped by Sprague. The trolley had caught on.

Like Tom Lowry in Minneapolis, businessmen in other cities became identified with the trolley industry. Though many citizens suspected them of manipulating railways for personal gain, many of the men who profited much from traction companies had business sensibilities that would have made them successful in any pursuit. The most interesting trolley magnates included Tom L. Johnson of Cleveland, Ohio; Henry E. Huntington of Los Angeles, California; and Charles Tyson Yerkes of Chicago, Illinois.

In 1879, Tom L. Johnson purchased Cleveland's Brooklyn Street Railroad and set out to develop it by means of a series of special promotions. One such enticement was a baseball game featur-

Open cars in Detroit's Cadillac Square

ing prizefighter John L. Lewis as pitcher, held at a ballpark Johnson had bought. By 1900, Johnson retired from business to go into politics. He was elected mayor of Cleveland in 1901 and was re-elected three times on a platform of "home rule, three-cent fares, and just taxation." As mayor, Johnson secured municipal ownership and operation of the city's street railway system.

In 1903, the city's two systems merged into the Cleveland Railway Company. Though the three-cent fare was not a successful measure and the system eventually fell into bankruptcy, the Cleveland Railway was reorganized in 1910 under a plan that provided good service, low fares, and reasonable returns to its owners. Ultimately, it developed into one of the United States' most progressive street railway systems. In the early 1920s, it claimed 1,500 streetcars, 415 miles of track, and 87 million passengers per year.

Another important railway of the time was the Los Angeles system. In the early 1890s, General Moses H. Sherman and his brother-in-law, Eli P. Clark, had organized the Consolidated Electric Railroad Company there. By 1895, they had electrified horsecar lines connecting Los Angeles to Pasadena, northeast of Los Angeles, and they later had electric cars running to Santa Monica, just west of the city. Their Los Angeles Pacific Railway supposedly doubled the size of the suburban cities along the beach within five years.

In 1898, Henry Edwards Huntington, nephew of the Southern Pacific's Collis P. Huntington, bought the Los Angeles Railway, as well as its rival, the Los Angeles Traction Company, which had been formed by Midwestern banker William S. Hook. In 1899, H. E. Huntington founded the Pacific Electric Railway, an interurban line that extended throughout most of southern California. Totally reworking the region's transportation system, he bought out old lines, built new ones, purchased new cars and equipment, and changed schedules and routes to improve them. To get more electricity for his trolleys, he became head of Pacific Light and Power Company.

Huntington's dream was a transit company that would unite the numerous cities around Los Angeles. "We will join this whole region into one big family," he declared, and he had considerable success in doing so. During its prime, the Pacific Electric Railway had more miles of track and earned more money per mile than any other electric interurban system in the world. It was then possible to commute quickly in the sprawling metropolis—twice as fast as a modern-day commuter can travel on buses through the congested traffic of the Los Angeles area. Interurban cars in southern California averaged 45 to 55 miles per hour, with few stops.

An important part of Los Angeles transportation for a good 40 years, Huntington's famed red cars seemed to be a way of life, used on all occasions. And they were particularly important in promoting real estate in southern California. Where new trolley tracks were laid, property was soon developed. Before Huntington's time, southern California consisted of isolated small towns. But after his transportation empire grew, those towns became "bedroom communities," tied to Los Angeles by virtue of housing many commuters. By 1910, when Huntington retired from active management of his traction properties, his system was known as "the world's greatest electric railway empire." At the time of his death in 1926, autos were already overwhelming Los Angeles, pushing trolleys out of business. But the familiar red trolleys had made an undeniable contribution to the growth of the city.

While the southern California railways grew, traction development was also taking place up the coast in San Francisco. Because the cable system was so successful in that hilly city, the development of electric railways was slow. After the 1906 earthquake and fire took their toll and destroyed much of the existing cable system, people decided it would be more efficient to put up trolley wire than to restore many of the cable cars. United Railroads of San Francisco, the principal San Francisco system during the period of electrification after the quake, ordered 200 new electric cars from the St. Louis Car Company. United Railroads was challenged by

the Municipal Railway of San Francisco, which was created by a
$2 million bond issue in 1909. But complete consolidation of San
Francisco street railway service did not take place until 1952.

Consolidation of independent streetcar companies was the rule
in most big cities, and Philadelphia was no exception. Between
1854 and 1895, that city had 66 street railway companies, but by
1895, most of them had been combined in the Union Traction
Company. In 1902, the Philadelphia Rapid Transit Company
brought the Union Traction Company together with the city's remaining surface and rapid-transit lines into a system that served
the entire metropolitan area. In 1911, financier E. T. Stotesbury
assumed control of the PRT and brought in Thomas E. Mitten, a
noted street railway manager, to oversee an expansion program.
Mitten subsequently extended lines into new areas, reorganized
routes, and improved labor relations. By 1923, the PRT had over
3,000 cars, 700 miles of track, and 900 million passengers per year.
In 1967, the company (by then known as the Philadelphia Transit

Philadelphia Rapid Transit Company cars on Chestnut Street

Trolleys at the corner of State and Madison in downtown Chicago, about 1910

Company) was still an important street railway operator, with 500 cars running on 12 routes.

One person who had bought into the streetcar lines of Philadelphia through two of that city's street railway magnates, named William Lukens Elkins and P. A. B. Widener, was Charles Tyson Yerkes. A Philadelphia native, he developed the street railway system of Chicago. After spending seven months in prison because of his involvement in a financial scandal, Yerkes came to Chicago in 1881, and in 1886, he entered the street railway field there. In that year, three companies owned the railways of the Windy City. The company operating on the south side consisted of cable lines, and the north and west side companies were made up of horsecar lines. Yerkes first got a 99-year lease on the north side company; he soon afterward got control of the west side company, and rebuilt both as cable systems.

In the years following 1886, Yerkes extended his service by building both cable and overhead trolley lines. He had a knack for being able to guess where the city's population would expand in forthcoming years. By 1898, Yerkes owned more than 500 miles of line and was known to many as "the greatest street railway mag-

A turn-of-the-century New Orleans City Railroad car at the corner of Carondelet and Canal Streets

nate in the West." But his cars were more showy than functional. Yerkes' strategy consisted of buying cheap equipment, fixing it up minimally, and selling it before it broke down.

An aggressive politician with a shady reputation, Yerkes built a machine with henchmen in both city and state government, as well as a strong public following. But in 1896, a printer, George E. Cole, began to wage a battle against Yerkes' corrupt politics, and Yerkes lost power in City Hall. Since his franchises were due to run out in 1903, he tried in 1897 to get one of his senators to introduce three bills that would take franchise-giving rights away from City Hall and give them to the legislature. When the newspapers publicized Yerkes' plan, the bills were killed in the house.

Consequently, by 1898, Yerkes' cronies were swept out of the city council and the legislature. He then concentrated on getting rid of his shoddy streetcar lines in order to leave Chicago. Organizing companies to take over the lines, he sold millions of dollars worth of stock. He contacted the street railway magnates he had known in Philadelphia, and they bought half the lines at the price he asked.

To them and to others, he sold the rest of the lines within two years. Yerkes left Chicago with nearly $20 million; he went later to London, where he built subways.

After Yerkes' departure, the two primary street railway systems of Chicago, the Chicago City Railway and the Chicago Railways Company, were granted franchise provisions and in 1913 were consolidated under the management of the Chicago Surface Lines. In the early 1920s, the company operated almost 3,500 streetcars on a network of 1,070 miles, transporting 1½ billion riders per year.

Chicago, Los Angeles, San Francisco, Philadelphia, Cleveland, and Boston are among the largest cities in the United States. But the trolley was by no means known only in those places. It was familiar to people in all areas, from all social classes, of all ages. Communities as diverse as Honolulu, Terre Haute, New Orleans, Buffalo, Chattanooga, and Denver had their own special trolleys, which they knew and loved. Post office trolleys, amusement park

Car no. 612 of New York Railways' "Green Lines" and three other Third Avenue Railway cars on joint trackage between Park and Madison Avenues, about 1910

excursion trolleys, street maintenance trolleys, funeral trolleys, private-parlor trolleys—vehicles that served a whole spectrum of purposes and tastes. For a time, the trolley was the only way to go.

A rapidly growing population and a spacious, open environment made trolleys flourish in the turn-of-the-century United States. But as technology developed, transportation evolved. Buses were cheaper to run, and management could change their routes without re-laying track. In big cities, subways proved practical. And surely the most dramatic change was the advent of the automobile as personal transportation. As cars became available to people of average income, trolleys were abandoned.

By World War II, other forms of transportation had replaced trolleys in most major cities of the United States. But the story of the trolley is a chapter of this country's history that will not be erased. The first form of motor-driven public transportation, trolleys did much to improve communication and facilitate trade, and they served as an important means of expanding cities. Thanks to them, people could live in rural areas and commute to urban jobs. Trolleys played an important part in the development of suburbs in many metropolitan areas.

It would not be an exaggeration to say that trolleys had a strong, direct influence on the homes and habits of average citizens. To many people, trolleys live on in memory, neither as inanimate machines nor as abstract historical forces, but as personal friends that accompanied them through the best and worst of times.

Convertible and semiconvertible cars pass under Memorial Day decorations in downtown Baltimore on May 28, 1919

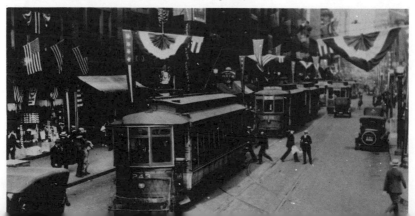

Bibliography

Adler, Cyrus. *Jacob H. Schiff—His Life and Letters.* New York: Double-day & Co., 1928.

Atwater, Isaac, ed. *History of the City of Minneapolis, Minnesota.* New York: Munsell & Co., 1893.

Cross, Marion E. *Pioneer Harvest.* Minneapolis: The Farmers and Mechanics Savings Bank, 1949.

Dreiser, Theodore. *The Titan.* New York: Crowell, 1974.

The Dual City Blue Book 1889-90. R. L. Polk & Co.

Eustis, William Henry. *The Autobiography of William Henry Eustis.* New York: James T. White & Co., 1936.

Hammond, John Winthrop. *Men and Volts—A History of General Electric.* Philadelphia: J. B. Lippincott Co., 1941.

Hudson, Horace B., ed. *A Half Century of Minneapolis.* Minneapolis: Hudson Publishing Co., 1908.

An Illustrated Historical Atlas of the State of Minnesota. Chicago: A. T. Andreas, 1874.

Kane, Lucille. *The Waterfall That Built a City.* St. Paul: Minnesota Historical Society, 1966.

Kieffer, Stephen. *Transit and the Twins.* Minneapolis: Twin City Rapid Transit Co., 1958.

Lowry, Thomas. *Personal Reminiscences of Abraham Lincoln.* London: Privately printed for Beatrice M. Lowry and her friends, 1910.

Martin, Albro. *James J. Hill and the Opening of the Northwest.* New York: Oxford University Press, 1976.

McDonald, Donna, ed. *Directory of Historical Societies and Agencies in the United States and Canada 1973–1974*. Nashville, Tennessee: American Association for State and Local History, and Maynard, Massachusetts: Inforonics, Inc.

Neill, Edward D. *History of Hennepin County and the City of Minneapolis*. Minneapolis: North Star Publishing Co., 1881.

Olson, Russell L. *The Electric Railways of Minnesota*. Hopkins, Minnesota: Minnesota Transportation Museum, Inc., 1976.

Rowsome, Frank. *Trolley Car Treasury*. New York: McGraw-Hill Book Co., 1956.

Shutter, Marion D., ed. *History of Minneapolis*. Chicago and Minneapolis: S. J. Clark Publishing Co., 1923.

Villard, Henry. *Memoirs of Henry Villard, Journalist and Financier, 1835–1900*. Boston: Houghton, Mifflin & Co., 1904.

Index

boldface pages contain illustrations

78; father of Clinton, 13–14, **15;**
real estate transactions of, 27, 28,
31, 34
Motor Line, **68,** 69, 87, 93, 94, 141

New Orleans, Louisiana, **168**
New York City, New York, 85, 89, 93,
161, **169;** as financial center, 57–59,
71, 112, 127, 130, 135, 139, 157;
Lowry in, 110, 112–116, 117, 124,
132–134
Nicollet House, 12, 45, 63
Nicollet Island, 47
Northrop, Cyrus, 65, 66–67, 71–72,
150
North Star Boot and Shoe Company,
29–30, 31
North Star Building, 29
Northwestern Guaranty Loan Com-
pany, 79, 124–125, 134
Northwestern Hospital for Women
and Children, 78–79
Northwestern Knitting Company, 79,
134
Northwestern National Bank, 36, 46,
65, **74,** 75, 79, 135

O'Brien, C. D., 65, 72
Oppenheim, Ansel, 59
Osgood, Philo, 36, 40
Ossanna, Fred, 157

panic of 1873. *See* Jay Cooke panic
panic of 1893, 123–124, 127–128, 132,
134, 152
Pavillion, 68
Philadelphia, Pennsylvania, **166,** 167,
168, 169
Pillsbury, Charles A., 46, 65, 69, 77,
79, 102, 134, 135
Pillsbury, George A., 65, 79
Pillsbury, John S., 53, 65, 66–67
Pillsbury-Washburn Flour Mills
Company, 129, 130
Pinney, Ovid, 19, 20
Pleasant View, Illinois, 3, 6, 153
politics, 4, 6, 7, 33, 82–83
power, 87, 93, 105, 161, 162; electric,
88–92, 93, 104, 117, 129; steam, 87,
144; water, 9, 13, 46, 129–130, 144

Prescott, Judge Amos, 38–40, 43
public library, 75–76

railroads, 38, 39, 67–68, 69, 82, 87,
109, 113; construction of, 9, 53, 54;
Lowry's interest in, 76–77
real estate, 3–4; in Minneapolis, 9, 11–
12, 48, 50, 51, 54, 63–64, 70, 78–
79; of W. S. King, 34, 38, 40, 124–
125; transactions made by Lowry,
17–21, 23–32, 81–82
Remington, Caroline A., 50
Remington, Eliphalet, 34, 35
Remington, Eliphalet III, 35
Remington, Philo, 35, 38–40, 43, 48–
50, 68, 69, 124–125
Remington, Samuel, 35
Remington family, 34–36, 87
Reminiscences of Abraham Lincoln
(Lowry), 7, 152
Republican Party, 33, 82, 83
Richmond, Virginia, 89–90, 100, 107,
161–163
Rushville, Illinois, 6

Saint Anthony, Minnesota, 11–12, 13,
47, 66
Saint Anthony Falls, 9, 39, 46, 67, 129
Saint Paul, Minnesota, 65, 85, 107,
110, 117, 161; and Lowry, 11, 81,
116, 150; and Minneapolis, 59–60,
66–67, 71–73, 119–120; growth of,
58, 59, 66, 131; streetcars of, 57–60,
104–105, 107, 115, 118, 130, 141,
145
Saint Paul and White Bear Railroad,
141
Saint Paul Chamber of Commerce, 60,
105
Saint Paul City Council, 104–105, 109,
110
Saint Paul City Railway Company, 81,
104, 105, 138; finances of, 85–86,
87, 109–116, 127, 134; organization
of, 57, 58–60
Saint Paul Medical School, 77
St. Thomas Seminary, 104
San Francisco, California, 165–166
Schiff, Jacob, 114, 115
Security Bank, 65

Goodrich Lowry, a grandson of Thomas Lowry, was born in Minneapolis in 1912. He was employed by the Northwestern National Bank of Minneapolis from 1936 until 1955, when he was elected president of the Northwest Bancorporation. He retired from banking in 1967 and has since followed a number of interests, including the early history of Minneapolis. He and his wife, Louisa, live in Wayzata, Minnesota, while their daughter, Jane, pursues an acting career in New York.

The text of this book was typeset in 11-point Baskerville. The chapter headings are in 16-point Baskerville Italic; the chapter numbers are in Tiffany Heavy; the book title is in Futura Display. The symbol that encloses the chapter numbers was used by the Twin City Rapid Transit Company (it contained the words *Twin City Lines*). The book was printed on 70# Ivory Carnival and bound in Kingston Natural Finish.